ALSO BY TEDDY WAYNE

The Love Song of Jonny Valentine
Kapitoil

LONER

Teddy Wayne

SIMON & SCHUSTER
New York   London   Toronto   Sydney   New Delhi

Simon & Schuster
1230 Avenue of the Americas
New York, NY 10020

This book is a work of fiction. Any references to historical events, real people, or real places are used fictitiously. Other names, characters, places, and events are products of the author's imagination, and any resemblance to actual events or places or persons, living or dead, is entirely coincidental.

First Simon & Schuster hardcover edition September 2016

SIMON & SCHUSTER and colophon are registered trademarks of Simon & Schuster, Inc.

For information about special discounts for bulk purchases, please contact Simon & Schuster Special Sales at 1-866-506-1949 or business@simonandschuster.com.

The Simon & Schuster Speakers Bureau can bring authors to your live event. For more information or to book an event, contact the Simon & Schuster Speakers Bureau at 1-866-248-3049 or visit our website at www.simonspeakers.com.

Interior design by Lewelin Polanco

Manufactured in the United States of America

10 9 8 7 6 5 4 3

Library of Congress Cataloging-in-Publication Data

Names: Wayne, Teddy, author.
Title: Loner : a novel / Teddy Wayne.
Description: New York : Simon & Schuster, 2016.
Identifiers: LCCN 2015044742 | ISBN 9781501107894 (hardcover) | ISBN 9781501107900 (softcover) | ISBN 9781501107917 (ebook)
Subjects: LCSH: College students—Fiction. | Man-woman relationships—Fiction. | Psychological fiction. | BISAC: FICTION / Literary. | FICTION / Psychological. | FICTION / Coming of Age. | GSAFD: Black humor (Literature)
Classification: LCC PS3623.A98 L66 2016 | DDC 813/.6—dc23 LC record available at http://lccn.loc.gov/2015044742

ISBN 978-1-5011-0789-4
ISBN 978-1-5011-0791-7 (ebook)

To Kate, and with her

Man can indeed do what he wants, but he cannot will what he wants.

—Arthur Schopenhauer, *Essay on the Freedom of the Will*

"After I go out this door, I may only exist in the minds of all my acquaintances," he said. *"I may be an orange peel."*

—J. D. Salinger, "Teddy"

LONER

Chapter 1

D avid," my mother said, "we're here."

I sat up straight as we passed through the main gate of Harvard Yard in a caravan of unassuming vehicles, rooftops glaring under the noonday sun. Police officers conducted the stammering traffic along the designated route. Freshmen and parents lugged suitcases and boxes heaped with bedding, posing for photos before the redbrick dormitories with the shameless glee of tourists. A pair of lanky boys sailed a Frisbee over the late-summer grass in lazy, slanted parabolas. Amid welcome signs from the administration, student banners interjected END ECONOMIC INEQUALITY, SILENCE IS VIOLENCE, and YALE = SAFETY SCHOOL.

A timpani concerto pounded in my chest as we made landfall upon the hallowed ground that had been locked in my sights for years. We'd arrived. I'd arrived.

"For the tuition we're paying," my father said, carefully reversing into a spot, "you'd think they could give us more than twenty minutes to park."

My parents climbed out of the car and circled around to the popped trunk. After tugging in vain at my door handle, I tapped on the window. "Where'd he go?" I could hear my mother ask.

"In here," I shouted, knocking louder.

"Sorry, thought you got out," my father said following my liberation. I checked in under a white tent teeming with my new classmates and received my room key and a bulky orientation packet. As we approached Matthews Hall, a girl emerged from the building. Seeing our hands were full, she paused to hold the door. I stepped inside and my orientation packet slid off the top of the box in my arms.

"Thanks," I said when she stooped down to get it.

"You would've been completely disoriented," said the girl, smiling, her nose streaked with contrails of unabsorbed sunscreen.

"She seems nice," my mother said encouragingly as we shuffled upstairs to the fourth floor. The doors were marked with signs listing the occupants and their hometowns, stamped with Harvard's *Veritas* shield. Beneath these were rosters of previous inhabitants, surname first. My room's read like an evolutionary time line of American democracy, beginning with a procession of gilded Boston Brahmins, gradually incorporating a few Catholics, then Goldbergs and Jacksons and Yangs and Guptas, and, in the 1970s, Karens and Marys and Patricias. My mother was impressed to discover an NPR correspondent on the list (I'd never heard of her). In fifty years, I thought, I'd humbly recall this moment in career-retrospective interviews, insisting that never in my wildest dreams did I imagine *my* name would someday be the one people noticed.

For the time being, though, I knew it didn't quite emblazon itself across the heavens like a verbal comet. David: blandly all-purpose, a three-pack of white cotton undershirts (CREWNECK, MEDIUM); Alan, an ulcerous accountant in Westchester circa 1957; then Federman, long *a* sound for the first vowel, an entity who is hardly here, or maybe he just left— Wait, who were we talking about, again? It was as if my parents, upon filling out my birth certificate, couldn't be bothered. *Tap is fine,* they always told waiters.

But now my ID card read *David Alan Federman, Harvard Student.*

My roommate, Steven Zenger, had yet to arrive. I claimed the front room, envisioning it would lead to impromptu visitors, a revolving door of campus characters popping in, lounging on my bed, gossiping late into the night.

My parents took my student card and fetched the remaining stuff as I unpacked. After setting down the final box, my lawyer father checked his watch. "Thirteen minutes," he announced, pleased with himself.

"Seven minutes to spare," my mother, also a lawyer, chimed in.

Through the door the hallway hummed with the chatter of other families.

"Well," said my mother, surveying the room. "This is exciting. I wish *I* were starting college again. All the interesting courses and people."

"And I bet you'll be beating the girls off with a stick," my father added. "There are a lot of late bloomers here."

My mother scowled. "Why would you say something like that?"

"I'm just saying he'll find his tribe." He turned to me. "You'll have a great time here," he said with the hollow brightness of an appliance manual congratulating you on your purchase.

"Just be yourself," my mother advised. "You can't go wrong being yourself."

"Yep." Sensing more imperatives and prophecies, I opened the door to let them out.

"Just one little thing, David," she said, raising a finger. "Sometimes when you talk, you do this thing where you swallow your words. I did it when I was younger, too. I think it comes from a place of feeling like what you say doesn't matter. But it's not true. People want to hear what you have to say. So try to enunciate."

I nodded.

"It helped me before I spoke to think of the word 'crisp,'" she said. "Just that word: *crisp*."

After our own swift hug, my mother prodded my father into initiating an avuncular, back-patting clinch. They seem comfortable enough with my sisters, but for as long as I can remember, my parents have acted slightly unnatural around me, radiating the impression of Good Samaritan neighbors who dutifully assumed guardianship following the death of my biological parents in a plane crash.

The door swung shut with a muted click. My bereft mattress and bookcase and motionless rocking chair stared at me like listless zoo animals. It was hard to picture people gathering here for fun, but a minute later someone knocked.

It was my mother.

"Your ID." She held out my student card. "It's very important— you can't open the door without it. Don't forget it again."

"I didn't," I said. "You guys did."

I resumed unpacking, yanking the price tags off a few items. Earlier that week my mother had dragged me to the mall, where I'd decided to adhere, for now, to my usual sartorial neutrality of innocuous colors and materials. It would serve me these first few weeks to look as benign as possible, the type of person who could be friends with everyone.

I was standing inside my closet, hanging shirts, when the door flew open and my roommate bounded into the room, his equally enthusiastic parents in tow.

"David!" he said. "Almost didn't see you. Steven." He walked over with his arm puppetishly bobbing for me to shake.

"If I look different from my Facebook photo, it's because I got braces again last week," he said. "But just for six months. Or five and three-quarters now."

All hopes I had of a roommate who would help upgrade me to a higher social stratum snagged on the gleaming barnacles of Steven's orthodontia. He would have fit right in at my cafeteria table at Garret Hobart High (named for New Jersey's only vice president), where I sat with a miscellaneous coalition of pariahs who had banded together less out of camaraderie than survival instinct. We were studious but not collectively brilliant enough to be nerds, nor sufficiently specialized to be geeks. We might have formed, in aggregate, one thin mustache and a downy archipelago of facial hair. We joked about sex with the vulgar fixation of virgins. We rarely associated outside of school and sheepishly nodded when passing in the halls, aware that each of us somehow reduced the standing of the other—that as a whole we were lesser than the sum of our parts.

While Steven's mother fussed over his room's décor, his father uncorked a geysering champagne bottle of hokey puns and jokes. "Matthews" became "math-use," so now "students can finally find out how learning math will help them later in life!" When his son remarked that the Internet in the dorms was free, Mr. Zenger chortled uncontrollably. "Free!" he roared, clapping his hands. "I didn't notice that when I wrote them a check last month! What a bargain! Free Internet!"

After a prolonged, maternally teary farewell—Mrs. Zenger smothered even me in her arms and assured me I was about to have the best year of my life—Steven invited me into his room. Nestled into a bean bag chair, he linked his hands behind his head, his collared shirt's elbow-length sleeves encircling hangman-figure arms.

"There's no lock on my door," he said. "So feel free to come in whenever you feel like hanging out."

"Okay," I said, lingering at the threshold.

"So what are you majoring in?" he asked. "I mean *concentrating* in," he threw in conspiratorially, now that we were in on the secret handshake of Harvard parlance.

"We don't have to declare until sophomore year, right?"

"Yeah, but I already know I'm going to concentrate in physics. How about you? What's your passion? What're you into?"

I was into success, just like everyone else who'd gotten in here, but admitting that was taboo. Though I'd excelled in all subjects, I didn't have the untrammeled intellectual curiosity of the true polymath. I was more like a mechanically efficient Eastern European decathlete grimly breaking the finish-line tape. Yet almost anyone could thrive in a field that consumed them. To lack ardor and still reach the zenith—that was a rare combination.

Because I never mentioned my grades to anyone and seldom spoke in class unless I had silently rehearsed my comments verbatim, my academic reputation never approached the heights of Alex Hines (yearbook prediction: *Fortune 500 CEO*), Hannah Ganiv (*poet laureate*), or Noah Schwartz (*President of the United States*). When the college acceptance list was posted, my classmates were shocked that I was our grade's lone Harvard-bound senior. (David Federman's yearbook prediction: *???* *FILL IN LATER*.)

But my teachers weren't. My letter of recommendation from Mrs. Rice made that much clear. (Eager to read her formal appraisal of my virtues, I overstated the number of copies I needed. When she handed me the stack of envelopes, I giddily retreated to the boys' bathroom, tore one open, and inhaled her praise like a line of cocaine in the fetid stall.) She wrote that I was "one of the most gifted students I have encountered in my twenty-four years teaching English at Garret Hobart High, already in possession of quite a fancy prose style (that sometimes goes over my head, I must admit!), although I can sense the immense strain human interactions put on him, whether in classroom discussions or individual conversations. It would be wonderful if David shared his observations more in class with his peers, who would surely benefit. But I have the utmost confidence that, with the properly nurturing environment, this young man, somewhat of a loner, will come out of his shell and be as expansive and eloquent in person as he is on the page."

I looked at Steven, the extroverted physicist in training, the trajectory of his impassioned career already plotted with a suite of differential equations he had memorized, his shell long since shucked.

"I guess I'm still waiting to really get into something," I said. "And if that doesn't happen, there's always a life of crime."

Steven waited a moment before laughing.

Later that afternoon, the two of us headed downstairs for an orientation meeting. Steven swatted the casings of all the doorframes we passed through and leapt the last three steps of each flight of stairs while holding the railing.

A few dozen freshmen mingled in the basement common room, key cards dangling over chests from crimson lanyards. Taxonomies hadn't been determined yet, hierarchies hadn't formed. We were loose change about to be dropped into a sorter that would roll us up by denomination.

"Lot of cute girls here," Steven said to me. He plopped himself on a couch and began chatting up a girl who wore a pink pair of those rubber shoes that individuate one's toes like gloves.

I took the seat on his other side. A number of "cute" girls did indeed dot the couches and folding chairs, even one or two who could compete with Hobart High's Heidi McMasters. (Our sole exchange, in eighth-grade earth science:

HEIDI: "Do you have a pen?"

DAVID: [*immediately hands her his best pen, never sees it again*])

A boy with chiseled forearms fuzzed with blond hair sat on the floor to my left. He was also not speaking to anyone, but seemed indifferent. I could tell he'd be popular.

"David," I said, extending my hand.

He shook it and looked around the room. "Jake."

"Are you from New York?" I asked, gesturing to his Yankees hat.

"Connecticut." His face lit up as he raised his hand. Another freshman swaggered up to him and slapped it. I introduced myself to the new guy.

"Phil," he said. They began talking about several people to whom they referred only by last names.

"You guys know each other from high school?" I asked.

"Same athletic conference," Phil said.

"Oh, what sport?"

"Baseball," he answered without looking at me.

Llabaseb, I thought—no, *llabesab.* I hadn't reversed a word in a month or two; I was getting rusty, far from the fluency of my younger years. At twelve, without many interlocutors to speak of (or to), I began a dialogue with language itself, mentally reversing nearly every word I encountered in speech, signs, objects I saw: *tucitcennoc* (Connecticut), *citelhta* (athletic), *draynal* (lanyard). Doing so came naturally—I'd visualize the word, reading it from right to left, syllable by syllable—and it surprised me when it impressed others. My verbal ability was discovered that year at summer camp, where for three days all the kids besieged me with requests to apply it to their names; Edward Park's was a crowd-pleaser. For those seventy-two hours I reveled in a social power I'd never had before, awaiting all the *gnolefil spihsdneirf* that would sprout from a few disordered words. Then the boy who could flip his eyelids inside out stole my thunder and, upon returning to the solitude of my parents' house, I graduated to a new lexical pastime: memorizing vocabulary lists in my older sister's SAT books. Words turned around in my mind only intermittently thereafter.

When the Harvard application solicited me to write about a meaningful "background, identity, interest, or talent," though, I was reminded of that summer I felt genuinely special. "To continuously reflect the world in a linguistic mirror," I postulated in the essay, "is to question the ontological arbitrariness of everything and everyone. Why is an *apple* not an *elppa*, nor, for that matter, an *orange*? Why am I *me* and not *you*?" I titled it "Backwords" and typed the whole thing in a reverse font and word order (by line), preparing to mail in a hard copy so that the reader needed to hold it up in front of a mirror. My parents, however, feared the admissions committee would think it was gibberish. Bowing to prudence, I compromised by writing the body of the essay normally and changing just the title to Ƨ◓ЯOWꓘↃAꓭ.

My "unique" essay had "rather intrigued" the Harvard admissions committee, my guidance counselor later informed me.

I waited for a lull in conversation between the baseball players. "Ekaj and lihp," I said.

"What?" Jake asked. "A lip?"

"Your names backward." They stared at me blankly. "Jake is 'ekaj,' Phil is 'lihp.'"

The two of them contemplated their reversed monikers and shared a look.

"Guess we're really at Harvard," Phil said under his breath.

I sank back into the couch's quicksand cushion, praying for the meeting to begin so that my silence wouldn't be conspicuous—or, failing that, for a monumentally distracting event: burst sewage pipe, freak hurricane, the president's been shot.

Uoy t'nac og gnorw gnieb flesruoy, I thought.

Someone tapped my shoulder and I turned around. "How was your move-in?" asked a girl standing behind the couch.

"I saw you coming into the dorm with your parents," she said after I failed to react. "I'm Sara."

"Oh, hi. David."

"Nice to remeet you."

"You, too," I said, and I was groping for something else to add when, from the entrance behind her, in the fashion of a queen granting a balcony appearance to the rabble below, you traipsed in, the nonchalant laggard. Suddenly there was no one else in the room; for the briefest of moments, as you entered my life, I paid myself no mind either, a rare, narcotic, unself-conscious bliss.

"You're late," Jake hollered in your direction. "You missed the meeting."

You glanced up from your phone. "Isn't it at four?" you replied.

He drew out the suspense for a beat. "Just messing with you."

You returned to your phone without any expression.

"It's about to start, though," he said. "Sit with us."

"Thanks," you said in a low, unmodulated voice. "I prefer to stand." You crossed to the other side of the room.

I'd received nothing from those fifteen seconds, but it felt like I had; Jake and Phil's loss was my gain. You had no truck with entitled athletes who chased openmouthed after fly balls like Labrador retrievers and assumed any girl would jump at the heliocentric opportunity to orbit their sun. Their assets from high school were liabilities here. *Guess we're really at Harvard,* I wanted to scoff in their faces.

Jake, looking unscathed by rejection, whispered something to Phil, who laughed.

"Well, I should probably find a place to sit," Sara said, and wandered off.

You sequestered yourself against a wall, arms crossed over your chest, the only student without a lanyard. You were here because it was compulsory, not to make friends. You had no interest in present company, didn't need to manufacture an affable smile and hope some generous soul took pity on you. No, you weren't one of us at all. You were in a tribe of your own.

How differently our lives would have unraveled over these years if the computer program generating the room assignments had started up a millisecond later, spat out another random number, and the two of us had never had a chance to meet.

Chapter 2

I f one were creating the Platonic ideal of a woman from scratch—which I could do here, manipulating the facts to serve my narrative agenda, though I'll cleave scrupulously to the truth—she would not necessarily resemble the being who had just swept through the common room, whose features I later had time to assess in magnified detail.

To begin with, your "flaws," a word I sandwich between petrified scare quotes. On the upper third of your forehead, as if connecting your two cerebral hemispheres, a blanched hyphen of a scar; a nose the tiniest bit crooked and long; two central incisors that outmuscled their next-tooth neighbors.

But the faces that are most compelling rarely belong to models, avatars of unblemished conventionality. They don't possess the imperfections that highlight the nearby superlatives—the distant twin mountains of an upper lip under an elegantly concave philtrum, the cheekbones sloping like the handle of a jug. And, most salient to an eye across a room, the hair in a carelessly knotted bun, a few rogue tendrils grazing the sides of your face, chestnut flecked with mid-October hues, a newly minted penny unsullied by commerce. That would be your hair-dye lyrical subcategory: "Mid-October." (My mother's color of choice is the law office sensible "Medium Ash Brown.")

My seat on the couch allowed me to study you with impunity while keeping the dorm proctor, a redheaded grad student in German philosophy, nearly in my sight line as he introduced himself. The heel of one of your leather-sandaled feet was planted against the wall. Gazelle legs encased in dark jeans; I estimated your height at a half inch shorter than mine, depending on our footwear. The spaghetti strap of a tank top climbed over lissome shoulders (a fuller bosom than your lemon-size breasts would have been incongruous— gauche, even—against your svelte torso). Adjacent to each strap was a pearly sliver of skin less touched by the sun; the rest was the tone of a patiently toasted marshmallow.

"One of the great things about college," the proctor said as my eyes remained on you, "is how seemingly unrelated stuff starts unifying in your mind. A theory you learn in a science lecture will connect to a line of poetry in your English seminar and link to a story a friend tells at lunch. Your world is expanding and diffusing while simultaneously contracting and growing denser. Everything, in a sense, becomes one thing."

After the abstract musings, he shifted to the practical matter of dorm rules, the details of which I would have been diligently committing to memory in my previous incarnation—the one that ended when you arrived. My concentration was broken only when the proctor, reading aloud the college's policy on sexual misconduct, suddenly lost his vocal footing.

". . . includes not only unwilling or forced vagin—vag—vag—"

His face turned a shade darker than his hair. I winced, but a few students snickered, Jake and Phil included, as he continued to trip on the word.

"—vag—vag—vag—" he stuttered, excruciatingly incapable of advancing, an oratorical Sisyphus. The poor guy, who'd likely spent years in speech therapy working to remedy a lifelong affliction, had finally decided he was ready to be in a position that required public speaking, and it was all undone with a single anatomical adjective before a room of puerile teenagers.

The more he persisted, though, the more my sympathy waned, replaced with resentment for his subjecting us all to such vicarious discomfort. Eventually he gave up, skipping the section altogether and moving on to the rules for alcohol and drugs.

I kept ogling brazenly without fear of detection until your head swiveled a few degrees from the proctor, casting, from your face to mine, an invisible string stretched taut.

It's difficult to say for sure, since I was less bold about looking at you after that, but I believe I was the only person you made eye contact with, however fleeting.

"That about wraps it up," the proctor said, flop-sweaty minutes after his slip-up. "Oh, whoops—I forgot the icebreaker game. Duh."

He asked us to go around in a circle and announce our first names prefaced by another word beginning with the same letter. I came up with a few options right away, to mitigate the anxiety of any turn-based speaking program, in which you count down with dread how many people are left until you, whereupon, as everyone looks your way, you must turn the key in the ignition of your vocal cords and hope they start without a hitch, always a risk with an inveterate mumbler in the final, shaky throes of puberty.

Adamant Adam, Terrestrial Tejas, Shy Sara, the attention of the room revolving with the centrifugal force of a roulette ball that was inexplicably gaining momentum. After my physics-passionate roommate proudly declaimed "Subatomic Steven," my mind went blank.

The room was still. Someone coughed.

As I tried to remember the words I had considered earlier, my internal dictionary scrubbed clean from *czar* to *each*, I heard, from the floor to my left, "Genius Jake." The others laughed in appreciation.

"We forgot David," Steven yelled.

All eyes reverted to me—yours included, I imagine.

"David," I squeaked. My brain harped on the word *vaginal*.

"Defiant," I said.

I was the only one to state my name before its alphabetical pairing—a small act of defiance itself, it occurred to me. I'd begun faultily but had recovered with verve, the gymnast sticking his landing after a herky-jerky dismount. I wondered if anyone else had taken note of my subversive maneuver.

"Funky-fresh Phil," said Jake's teammate as the room again buckled in laughter. The line approached you.

"Veronica," you said in your voice with nothing to prove, so unlike my own timorous quaver. Then, with the minutest upturning of the left side of your lip, "*Veritas.*"

You were the only person who had followed my lead. Kindred spirits of swapped syntax. And, from that curling lip, there was some mischief to your appropriation of our college's motto of truth.

Other names and parts of speech skittered around as the game continued, but I heard only the two words you had spoken. Had you gone standard as everyone else had—*Vivacious Veronica*—it's possible that you would not have lassoed my imagination so completely, that I might have feasted on your superficial appeal over the course of that meeting and decided I was sated. Yet that Latin addition meant you had more than beauty in your arsenal. You possessed creativity and wit and, as your dismissal of jockstrap Jake and feeble-minded Phil had suggested, valued intelligence and sensitivity.

Veritas: someone like me had a shot. We were, after all, really at Harvard.

When the meeting concluded Steven drafted me into a six-person troupe he had formed in the scrum of the common room. We trundled over for dinner to Annenberg Hall, that cathedral-like space splashed across the brochures and websites, where glowing, ethnically diverse faces rounded out every photo. I'd seen it during my campus visit with my father a year earlier, but tonight I was no longer a mere spectator of its burnished walnut paneling, stained-glass windows, and chandeliers; I was standing in the brochure it-self, ready for my close-up.

I brought my tray over to the table Steven had secured. As was my New Jersey set, they were a visual hodgepodge, a chimera of the shambling (Justin) and the husky (Kevin) and the ectomorphic (Steven), the overdressed (Carla looked like she was on her way to a college interview) and the flamboyantly unfashionable (Ivana and her shoe gloves), topped off by an aggressively nondescript seat filler (Sara, who had gravitated to us).

Sara patted the empty chair next to her. "Saved you a seat," she said.

Though an upgrade over my Hobart High lunch club—three girls!—we were still clearly freshmen who had missed out on the normal high school experience and were now attempting to simu-late it in college. Our dinner conversation revolved around the cui-sine, the refuge of those with little in common. We lobbed insults at the sogginess of the tater tots. We mocked the desiccation of the halal grilled chicken. We speculated about breakfast. Everyone re-sponded to each joke like soused nightclub patrons yukking it up as a legendary comedian trotted out his greatest hits.

I forced myself to smile along, but felt a spasm of apprehen-sion seeing the next few months unfolding much like this, the ripe cranberry blush of autumn fading to bleached December. By cruel accident, these might well become my college friends. We would choose to live together as upperclassmen, visit one another on va-cations, stay in touch after graduation, attend the other members' nuptials—maybe two of us would even get married. We would rate the hors d'oeuvres at the wedding reception and ponder what brunch would be.

My cowardly instinct was to cling to them. But not for too long: powerful clans are never this diverse and scattered. Only the outcast are.

I got up to scoop myself a bowl of sugary cereal amid the symphony of fork tines scraping white ceramic plates, wending past tables populated by students who appeared to have happily found their tribes: girls with chemically blond hair; an octet of preppy black students; football behemoths with phalanxes of neon sports drinks; chicly dressed Asians; outdoorsy types toting bumper-stickered Nalgene bottles; future Undergraduate Council presidents and their cabinet members; legacy WASPs with Roman numerals appended to their names and swoops of hair soldered to their foreheads.

When I sat back down, there you were at last, coming into the dining hall late.

You stood in the roped-off line near my table among the clutch of students you'd arrived with, engaged in a whispery tête-à-tête with another girl, already having things worth saying in confidence. The rest of your group possessed a similar ease, as though they'd hung out together for years. A uniformity of physical desirability differentiated by grace notes: that girl's raven tresses and alabaster skin against your coppery tones, that boy's cultivated stubble, the one black guy wearing a gauzy scarf in August. I watched them—you, really—in slow motion, cinematographer of the hackneyed movie sequence in which the cafeteria's din silences and a languorous song spills in as your moving lips swallow up the frame.

I could tell that you all had not only gone through high school as one should but had done so precociously in seventh and eighth grades; your secondary education had featured the unfettered experimentation typically associated with college; and now you were, compared with the rest of us, bona fide adults.

One other thing was obvious, from your clothes, your body language, the impervious confidence you projected, as if any affront would bounce off you like a battleship deflecting a BB pellet: you came from money.

My parents made good salaries practicing law, but nothing close to the assets of your families, where a crack about tuition and parking would never even come to mind, let alone be verbalized. Yet your crowd didn't reveal its class by stock emblems of affluence: navy blazers with brass buttons and chinos, pearl necklaces, the plumage of those crimson-and-blue-blooded WASPs who looked like they'd been born wearing a pair of boat shoes. Yours was subtler and pitted against that bloated, decaying archetype. You had traveled widely, dined at Michelin-starred restaurants without parental supervision, matriculated at schools with single-name national reputations, ingested designer drugs and maybe had a cushy stint in rehab.

It wasn't just your financial capital that set you apart; it was your worldliness, your taste, your social capital. What my respectable, professional parents had deprived me of by their conventional ambitions and absence of imagination.

I'd done everything I was supposed to my whole life, played by all the rules. It had gotten me into Harvard, but look where I was sitting: with Subatomic Steven and the rest of our lost-and-found bin.

As I hovered over my bowl of Lucky Charms with soy milk, your conversation with the girl concluded. You took an eyedropper out of your pocket, reclined your head, and squeezed a couple of times into both sides. Then you closed your eyes and massaged the corners, as if the public world were too pedestrian to bear witness to and necessitated a retreat into your private one. You blinked several times, your eyes glassy with artificial tears, and stared off into space. It seemed like we were the only two people in the cacophonous dining hall not speaking to anyone, the only two not fully present.

A moment later the ID checker asked for your card. You were

still in your stupor, and one of your friends nudged you. You snapped out of it with a halfhearted laugh. I then understood. Maybe you wouldn't admit to it, maybe you didn't even know it yet, but you were also faking it. Somewhat of a loner, too.

Justin and Kevin were hosting a gathering in their suite that night. When Steven was ready to go, I told him that, actually, I was pretty exhausted.

He insisted I come. "You don't want to miss out on the first night," he said. "Someday we'll all reminisce about it."

Precisely. But the immediate terror of staying in while everyone else on campus drank alcohol together and hooked up—my four years of high school compressed to one joyless evening—began to eclipse my fears of the long-term consequences.

"Maybe for a bit," I said.

Crudely Scotch-taped to the walls of Kevin's bedroom was a gallery of posters for comedies and gangster movies starring all-male ensembles. A purple tapestry tacked to the ceiling cast everything in a dank submarine light.

Justin's height—a slouch-shouldered six foot five—and fake Idaho ID had enabled him to purchase thirty-six cans of beer and two plastic jugs of vodka from a liquor store in Central Square. I splashed orange juice into my cup of vodka and took a sip. An acrid corruption of my breakfast beverage of youth. I'd have to find something more palatable, a signature drink.

Everyone was more reserved in the cloistered intimacy of a dorm room. When the conversation remained stilted, Ivana suggested we play the drinking game Never Have I Ever.

"Never have I ever blacked out from drinking," she said after a cursory review of the rules.

"I'm confused," Steven piped up, unashamed to put his ignorance on display. "You haven't blacked out yourself, but if someone else has, they drink?"

Justin and Kevin nodded and swigged from their cups with lupine grins of self-satisfaction, conquests masquerading as confessions.

On Carla's turn, she brought up marijuana use. Kevin, Justin, and Ivana all drank. I'd seen it just once in person, when a drum-playing skater had passed a green baggie to his friend under a desk before history class.

"Never have I ever been fingered by someone," said Kevin.

The sudden swing into the crassly sexual startled us all, except Ivana, who tipped her cup, emboldening Carla to follow suit and rendering Sara the female holdout. She peered into the opening of her beer can while everyone else stayed silent.

My lower back prickled with perspiration. I hadn't even kissed a girl yet, an abyss of experience I'd hoped never to reveal at all in college, and certainly not on the first night.

My turn. To head off any further declarations of carnal milestones, I said, "Never have I ever been convicted of a felony," knowing that none of us teachers' pets had ever run afoul of the law and hoping it would act as a reset button which, as an ancillary benefit, would shift the focus from Sara's contagious embarrassment. No one drank. From there things amplified into the absurd: orgies, snorting cocaine off strippers' breasts, unsolved homicides. The game petered out, followed by a card trick from Steven (he'd brought his own deck).

We split up into factions. Sara ended up next to me on the bony futon and we traded getting-to-know-you questions. She was planning to concentrate in Latin American history; she'd gone to a magnet school in Cleveland; she had an older brother and younger sister.

I didn't have much to say about my sisters when Sara asked. Miriam had been genuinely apathetic to me growing up and had recently decamped across the country for law school, cohabitating with the boyfriend she'd had since college. Anna spent all her time socializing; when she and I overlapped in my senior year at Hobart High, I tacitly agreed never to speak to her in the hall lest I betray our relation. I'd always envied the brothers and sisters whose last names were legendary among the student body—those handsome Wilson boys, the wild Capalleri sisters. The entirety of Anna's farewell to me the morning I left for college, after my parents woke her, was an irritable "Bye" shouted from her bed. Those crazy three-to-four-years-apart Federman siblings.

"My older sister's in law school and my younger one's in high school," I told Sara.

"How old are they, exactly?" Before I could answer, she laughed. "I'm the worst at small talk. You must be so bored. Hey, here's a fun fact: I spell my name without an *h*."

"I spell *David* with two *d*'s," I said. "I'm even worse at small talk."

"No." Then, with robotic caesurae and emotionless inflection: "I—am—worse."

"I believe—I am—in fact—worse," I said in the same voice.

"I—dis—a—gree," said Sara. "De—fi—ant—ly."

Defiant: my nominal adjective. I tried to remember hers—*short? sensitive? shy!*—but her phone rang. "Sorry," she said before picking it up and leaving the room. "My parents."

On the floor by my feet, poking out under a men's magazine promising its reader guns for biceps, was Harvard's *Freshman Register*, known as the Facebook, onetime inspiration for the digital Goliath. I hadn't picked up my copy yet. I flipped through the *F*s.

There he was: David Alan Federman, wearing a white dress shirt, tie, and yearbook-photographer-mandated smile—a rectangular vacuum of charisma. My hair the drabbest of browns, destined to desaturate without distinction, parted like a small-market weatherman's. My complexion was barely contrastable from the shirt and white space bordering the frame. Features that neither enticed nor repelled. A body sixty-eight and three-quarters inches long and 146 pounds at my last checkup, outwardly average in all respects.

The museum card next to the artwork: *Garret Hobart High School, 152 Midvale Ln.*, my hometown, the humiliating two letters of *NJ*.

Turning to the first-name index in the back, I found two Veronicas. The first wasn't you. The second was in the middle of the *W*'s, above a spare Park Avenue address and *The Chapin School*, a faceted blue sapphire among the round gray pebbles:

Veronica Morgan Wells.

Careless sunglasses half hidden in windswept hair, a collared shirt with just enough pearl-snap buttons unfastened to make your décolletage inviting but not tawdry. Behind you, an indeterminate bifurcation of sea and sky, your serenely unimpressed smile implying the background was a perennial vacation spot rather than a one-off outing. You had wrapped up a day of lounging in a secluded cove on a private beach, reading a Russian novel from a clothbound volume, wondering how you could feel so lonely in such a beautiful place—you'd always worried there was something defective about you, were scared people wouldn't like you when they got to know the real you, maybe you'd meet someone at Harvard who would accept you for who you were, and next summer you could take him back here.

(I'd spent July and August interning at my father's law office in a squat brick building that shared a lobby with Dr. Irving Jomsky, chiropractor.)

Sara came back and I casually tossed the *Register* on the floor. Carla joined us and talked about Freshman Week activities, but all I could think about, running in a loop, was Veronica Morgan Wells, Veronica Morgan Wells, Veronica Morgan Wells. The quadrisyllable that halves its beats at the middle name, dividing again at its pluralized terminus of subterranean depths. The percussively alert *c* drowsily succumbing to the dozing *s*. Perfectly symmetrical initials, the *V* found twice upside-down in the *M*, inverted once more in the *W*, and, if spoken, easily confused with a German luxury automaker.

Sara talked about participating in the First-Year Urban Program for preorientation, whose main project had been "reconstructing furniture for low-income families in Boston."

"I was pretty bad at it," she admitted. "I think I ended up *de*constructing the furniture, to be honest. I was like the team's Derrida." She waited for us to laugh at the reference that neither of us yet knew. "You guys do any programs?"

"The Fall Clean-Up with Dorm Crew," Carla said.

"I didn't know about that option," said Sara. "That sounds fun. What did you guys clean up?"

"Mostly bathrooms in the dorms. The pay was good, though."

"Oh," Sara said, clearly discomfited by the socioeconomic schism. "David, how about you?" she asked, her eyes meeting mine pleadingly.

"I stayed home," I said.

I returned to my room shortly thereafter. In my bed, I sleuthed around the warrens of the free! Internet for your name, adding information from the *Register* (high school, address), modifying it with new data that cropped up (on the track team, with three-thousand-meter race times recorded in a few places; supporting cast in some plays and then, senior year, Lady Macbeth in your girls' school's production; a quote in a news item on Chapin's website about your participation in Model UN: " 'It's a wonderful opportunity for students to think about the world outside themselves,' said junior Veronica Wells, representing Hungary."). Progenitors: Lawrence, member of the senior brass at a household-name financial services firm and a Harvard Business School graduate, and Margaret, who, according to the *New York Times*, "sits on the board of various philanthropic organizations," and whose willowy figure was photographed on a host of society websites. No siblings I could find.

And no other photos, except perhaps for those cached in your

Facebook page, which was off-limits to me. (I couldn't locate any additional social media accounts in your name.) You'd used the same profile picture as in the *Register*. I saved it to my computer and zoomed in.

You had no affiliation with Steven's modest metric of *cute*. Cute didn't fuel Romeo and Dante and Paris, couldn't galvanize the unerring belief that their inamorata justified any sacrifice, that their quest for Juliet or Beatrice or Helen, successful or not, was itself a peerless achievement reflecting back on their own valor. There's just one Everest, and only the most heroic can reach the summit.

You'd elected not to list your dorm room or any contact details in the student directory, so I combed the doors on my floor. I didn't find your name and went upstairs. It was at the end of the hall, on room 505, a symmetrical number to match your symmetrical initials.

Yours was also a two-person suite. Headlining the sign was SARA COHEN, CLEVELAND, OH. Sara without an *h*.

Chapter 3

I looked around for you on campus over the next few days, a blitz of tours, placement tests, and advisory meetings. With my placeholder friends, I endured a marathon of organized social outings: the Tin Man gyrations of the First Chance Dance; the Freshman Talent Show, dominated by music and juggling performances (Steven put on a well-received magic act); the annual screening of *Love Story*, interrupted with increasingly tedious commentary from Crimson Key members, the student group that ran much of Freshman Week; the A Cappella Jam, exactly as fun as it sounds. You were a consistent no-show. Sara, too, refrained from most activities.

To lend my bare walls some color, I bought a van Gogh print of sunflowers. After affixing it with dorm-approved putty, I recognized I was becoming a collegiate cliché and returned to the Harvard Coop, but saw that no matter what I might purchase—Dalí's *The Persistence of Memory*, Munch's *The Scream*, the couple kissing in Times Square, John Belushi in his COLLEGE sweatshirt, a kitten doing its best to *hang in there*—I'd at best be some potpourri of stereotypes.

Hence I decided to transform my room into a self-aware caricature by full-throttling van Gogh, plastering the wall above my bed with a collection of his most famous yellow-hued paintings to complement the original sunflowers: a chair, café exteriors, straw hats, whorled wheat fields. I stood back and admired the results with a chuckle. (If anyone ever noticed my thematic curation, they didn't say anything.)

When the opportunity presented itself, I made a few bumbling attempts to strike up conversations with other freshmen. None backfired as badly as with Jake and Phil, but they never led to anything, either. It was still better, I reasoned, to bide my time with my entryway companions than to sit by myself like a leper, and so I stuck with the clique, who had christened themselves the Matthews Marauders.

"We're pregaming in our room again at eight o'clock," Justin announced the fourth night at dinner.

"Technically speaking, we rarely go to any games," Steven said. "So we're stretching the definitional properties by calling it pregaming."

"Who cares? The pregaming's the best part," said Kevin. "Not gonna lie: the actual game usually sucks."

"Yeah," Justin agreed. "If I spent my whole life just pregaming with you guys and never going to any games, I'd be cool with that."

"Once we start going to parties," Kevin proposed, "we should just think of *them* as pregaming for some other game."

Justin raised his glass of soda. "To pregaming and never gaming."

"Puk-chh," said Kevin as he jerked his arm in two movements to toast with Justin. He punctuated much of his speech with sound effects of cinematic violence: guns loading and firing or cyborg combatants landing bone-pulverizing punches.

"You guys crack me up," Ivana said, shaking her head fondly. "You're so weird."

They weren't, in the slightest. They were completely ordinary, all of them, having already pledged their fealty to one another halfway through the first week of college, with no aspirations to maraud beyond the claustrophobic perimeter and dirty-sock musk of Justin and Kevin's room.

Sara ate meals with us, but sat out the pregame sessions with various excuses: early wakeup for a meeting, scheduled phone call with her grandmother. She hadn't referred to a long-distance boyfriend or other freshmen she'd befriended, so it appeared that she was just reclusing in her room. Or in her room with you. Perhaps she, too, saw our group as a parochial small town and was scheming to flee it with her roommate as her one-way Greyhound ticket—in which case I needed to guarantee I was also on board.

My only sightings of you were in the dining hall, where your friends had claimed a table in a far corner yet managed to make themselves the hub of attention and activity, with other social blocs frequently coming by to pay their respects, as if your preeminent coastal provenance had been directly transposed onto the map of Annenberg and the rest of us were flyover country. Over the course of the week I'd seen enough of their faces to locate the core members' entries in the *Freshman Register*. Their footprints on the Internet were private or contained no tangential material about you. A few were from Los Angeles or abroad, but most had attended prep schools in New York. That explained your immediate alliance— your social scopes were not limited to your high schools but encompassed small-world networks of the well-heeled: second homes, clubs, family connections. That, or you'd simply identified your kin on sight, and if I ever attempted to breach your city walls, you would instantly peg me as a barbarian.

Sitting at lunch one day with the Matthews Marauders, I was furtively reading an essay from that morning's *Crimson* about the author's attempts to squelch her inborn competitiveness with her classmates over grades, summer internships, and boyfriends. ("Then I realized," she wrote in the generously italicized and disingenuous epiphany, "that I didn't have to be *the best*. I just had to be the best *me*.")

"Let's start the pregaming half an hour earlier tonight," Kevin said. "We may as well maximize our hangout time together before classes start."

"Fine by me—I can't get enough of your guys' dumb jokes," Ivana said teasingly.

"Yeah, right," Justin said. "You know they're hilarious."

I imagined one of the hulking chandeliers above us breaking free and crashing on our table in a blizzard of glass.

When I tilted my head back down, I spotted you grabbing two pears from a basket and walking to the exit, none of your private-school mafia in the vicinity. A chance to stage a seemingly random encounter.

I abandoned my partially eaten lasagna on the dishwasher track and followed you outside, maintaining a discreet distance as you cut across Harvard Yard. The chiming of the Memorial Church noon bells was drowned out by the sputtering roar of a lawn mower. A monarch butterfly juked flirtatiously in front of me. You were biting into one of the pears and heading toward Matthews. I could enter with you, make you aware that I lived in the same dorm, maybe jokingly remind you of our shared name-first, descriptor-second introductions that night in the common room.

You got waylaid by something written in chalk on the pavement. I swerved around you and over to Matthews, where I waited by the entrance, pretending to be immersed in my phone. When you approached, I pushed the door open and held it. Up close, your skin appeared like the unperturbed shell of some creamy European confection.

"Thanks," I said, flustered, as you stepped in.

I'd mixed it up; I was the one doing something for you. I would've been better off making the bad pun I'd formulated during my chase: *Pair of pears?*

Yet the verbal blunder didn't offset my small chivalrous gesture. You smiled at me. Not the coy smile of your Facebook photo—a genuine one, flashing the full range of your front teeth.

It was like entering Harvard Yard again on move-in day. Cue the timpani.

Not wanting to seem as if I were tailgating you upstairs, I loitered in the lobby, browsing the fliers on the bulletin board. "Stressed or sad?" one read. "Anxiety and depression are the two most common mental health diagnoses among college students. Schedule an appointment with university health services today."

"Harvard isn't for everyone," my guidance counselor had told me in my junior-year advising session, words I ignored as boilerplate dissuasion he dispensed to every Cambridge hopeful in hedging against the school's stingy acceptance rate. "It's true that it can open doors for you later, but you might well get a richer college experience elsewhere, in a place you can find yourself more easily. This is often the problem when you go somewhere primarily for its name."

It's convenient, in hindsight, to blame Harvard. But it wasn't the guilty party.

Chapter 4

The eve of Harvard's weeklong shopping period, in which students sample classes before selecting them, I was on my bed, laptop scalding my thighs, meandering the Internet of you, looking at the photo and cycling through the same information. (" 'It's a wonderful opportunity for students to think about the world outside themselves,' said junior Veronica Wells, representing Hungary.")

The September breeze carried boisterous shrieks and distant music up to my open window. The Matthews Marauders were in the Yard, attending the Ice Cream Bash. (As with the A Cappella Jam, a number of social happenings attached an overblown noun that leached them of any allure: the Foreign Students Fete, the Hillel Gala.) I didn't have it in me to go to yet another cornpone event, especially when you were unlikely to be present.

An e-mail pipped into my in-box among the deluge of university mass mailings. It was from Daniel Hallman, a charter member of my high school cafeteria table. He was reporting on his first week at the University of Wisconsin, where, he claimed, he'd gotten "wasted or high" every night and had received "blow jobs from three girls, though not at the same time . . . yet."

His tone was unrecognizable, nothing like the Daniel of the previous four years, who once in a while threw in a sly remark at lunch, who had never, to my knowledge, had a real conversation with a girl outside of class. Though he was evidently a new man now, flush with alcohol in his bloodstream and treatable venereal diseases, to engage with him, albeit electronically, would be to return to that cafeteria table, an even more desperate seat than my current one in Annenberg.

Yet *he* was the one having the quintessential college experience, drunkenly bed-hopping, while I had locked myself up in sober solitary confinement. I thought of my childhood bedroom, the years in which no one other than family members and cleaning ladies had set foot inside it. It occurred to me that, had I not been assigned a roommate, I could die on my twin mattress and it might take weeks until someone investigated.

My phone buzzed.

"So he *does* know how to use that expensive device we bought him," my mother said after I picked up.

"Sorry for not calling back." I could hear NPR in the background. "You're in the car?"

"We're going out for Chinese. I didn't feel like cooking." She lowered the radio. "So? How are you? How's Harvard?"

"It's okay," I said. "Classes haven't started yet."

"And your roommate? What's he like?"

"He's fine. I don't think we're going to be best friends or anything."

"No?" She sounded disappointed. To my father: "Green light." Back to me: "Well, it takes time to get to know some people. I'm sure once classes begin you'll make a few friends."

"I have friends already," I said. "There's a bunch of us in the dorm that eat together every meal and hang out. The Matthews Marauders."

"Really?" she asked. "That's great. What about that nice girl we met moving in?"

"Sara," I said. "She's in the group, too. We talked awhile the other night."

"Oh, good. I liked her."

We both waited for the other to say something.

"But things are okay?" she asked.

"Yeah." My voice cracked. I took a drink of water from a stolen Annenberg cup. "Really good, actually. I even have a nickname everyone calls me. David Defiant."

"Anna, put your phone on silent," she chided. "Sorry, what did you say? They call you David Definite? Why's that?"

"Defi—it's a long story."

"You'll have to tell it to me sometime," she said. "Listen, we just got to the restaurant, but I'm glad to hear you're enjoying yourself."

"I should go, too."

"Oh? What're you doing tonight?"

The bass from the Ice Cream Bash turned up. "I'm going to this ice cream party."

"Sounds fun," she said. "Remember to take your Lactaid."

Hordes of students ate ice cream from paper cups, gabbing amiably as sanitized pop music played on speakers. While no one was looking, I swallowed one of the two lactose-intolerance pills I stored at all times in the small fifth pocket of my jeans, entered the fray, and got in line. It seemed like I was the only untethered attendee, as if everyone else knew the secret that ensured they were never alone at a party.

"Hello?" The Crimson Key member wielding the scooper was looking at me with hostile impatience under his perky mask. "What can I get you?"

I quickly asked for vanilla. "No, wait," I said as he plunged his arm into the bucket. Vanilla was what I always picked, the gastrointestinally safe base that deferred flavor to its toppings.

"Chocolate," I revised. "With rainbow sprinkles, please."

I was tucking into my audacious dessert, wondering how long I could last without speaking to anyone, when Sara materialized in another well-timed intervention. She wore a capacious L.L.Bean backpack and was empty-handed.

"No ice cream?" I asked.

"I was hoping there'd be sorbet. I'm pretty lactose intolerant." She added, with mock solemnity, "We all have our crosses to bear."

The spare lactase-enzyme supplement bulged in my pocket. I reached in and fingered its single-serving packet. To offer it to her would be an admission that we together were fragile Jews in the crowd, unable to stomach a treat little kids gobbled unthinkingly.

"Here," I said quietly, handing her the packet as if making a drug deal. She recognized what it was and smiled.

"Thanks," she said, tearing it open and depositing the pill on her tongue. I felt a curious surge of warmth toward her.

We drifted back to the ice cream table. "So, a fellow digestively challenged Ashkenazi," she said. "You *are* Jewish, right? Your last name sounds like you're a member of the tribe."

"Uh-huh," I said. "You haven't been around in a while. Were you in hiding?"

"Ah, you've seen through my facade," she said. "Underneath this pleasant exterior lies a deeply antisocial personality. I'm a closet sociopath. Or psychopath, I mean. I always confuse them."

She chuckled. I spooned some ice cream into my mouth and nodded.

"Groups aren't my thing," she went on, waving her hand at the masses around us. "I'm an extroverted introvert at best. But everyone says that, right? They want to claim the best parts of each—that they can be charming when they need to, but they really prefer solitude. No one's ever, like, 'I have the neediness of an extrovert and the poor social skills of the introvert.' Sorry I'm talking so much. I've been in the library all day prepping for my freshman seminar."

"I'm not that good in groups, either," I said, thinking of Mrs. Rice's letter of recommendation. "Or one-on-one."

She laughed authentically.

"Like, when it's just Steven and me in the room, I'm not any more comfortable than I am here." It was a clunky segue to my next question. "Who's your roommate?"

"Veronica Wells? The really pretty girl?"

Feigning ignorance, I shook my head. "I haven't been paying much attention to the people in our dorm. Is she nice?"

"I wouldn't know," Sara said. "I've seen her maybe five times. I think the last conversation we had was when she turned on the light at four in the morning and said, 'Sorry.' "

"Oh, you're also in the front room," I said. "That's annoying, huh?"

She shrugged.

"So do you have any sense of her?" I was leading the witness ham-fistedly, but I couldn't stop myself.

"Not really. She and her crowd seem a bit too-cool-for-school."

"Does she have gatherings in your room?"

"No, thank God."

A spastic "Hey, guys!" interrupted us. It was Steven, in the second physics-pun T-shirt he'd worn that week (MAY THE M•A BE WITH YOU).

With breathless excitement, he informed us that there was a proctor in Grays who wasn't cracking down on freshman parties, and they were having a big one tonight, the other Marauders were being lame, but did we want to come?

"I'd better stay in," Sara said, taking a skittish step back.

You and your too-cool-for-school friends might be there, at an unsanctioned event. Sara and you clearly weren't friends, but she could nevertheless provide a bridge, rickety though it was. And thus far hardly anyone else was even talking to me.

"C'mon," I said. "I thought groups were your thing. What are you, a closet psychopath?"

The reference was just enough of a gesture toward intimacy to elicit a giggle. Parroting something a person had previously said in a different context, I was figuring out, was a winning tactic. The subject is flattered you paid such close attention in the first place and commends her own intelligence for catching the allusion.

"When in Rome," she said, hands clenching the straps of her backpack like a soldier preparing to parachute into enemy territory.

Inside the rain forest fug of the dorm room, we leaked through a strainer of bodies toward a desk that had been transformed into a bar. I poured myself half a cup of gin and glazed it with tonic water; Sara reached into a cooler of beer cans bobbing in a slushy bath. A poster of Bob Marley exhaling miasmically presided over the festivities. Clubby music blared a beat resembling a spaceship's self-destruct alarm.

I scanned the room. You weren't there. But it was early.

Steven ambled off to find some people he knew; he had already gotten himself elected mayor of Harvard's nerdy township, of which the Matthews Marauders was one of many districts.

Sara and I were left alone. In between baby sips of her beer, she confessed she'd hardly drunk alcohol before this week.

"I wasn't what you'd call Miss Popular in high school." She wiggled the tab on her beer can like a loose tooth. "Unless 'mispopular' became a word. Thank God for Becky and Ruma. Those were my two best friends."

I had always envied the depth of female friendships—even the abjectly ostracized seemed to have a soul mate on the margins with them. I'd have traded that for my tenuous coterie of fools.

"I was sort of the same," I said. "I had two hundred classmates, and I bet half of them wouldn't even remember me."

The tab on Sara's can snapped off and, with no garbage nearby, she slipped it into her pocket. "But the anonymity is kind of nice," she reflected. "I always felt a little sorry for the kids at the top. Everyone's watching them. That can't be easy. If no one's paying attention to you, at least you can be yourself, do your own thing."

I was about to counter that whatever things the anonymous accomplished, they were of little consequence, since nobody noticed. But she had a point. Unseen, you could take your time, slowly amass knowledge and skills. For years everyone could believe you were a faceless foot soldier; they hadn't investigated more closely, or they simply lacked the necessary powers of discernment. Then, in a single stroke, you could prove them all wrong.

Someone jostled my arm as he passed, spilling gin and tonic on my wrist.

"No one paying attention to you." I licked my sticky skin like a cat. "I guess that's something I identify with."

"Something *with which* you identify," she said playfully. "Aren't you glad you're talking to that fun girl at the party who reminds you to never end a sentence on a preposition?"

"You should also try to never split an infinitive," I said, but whoever was manning the volume control cranked it up and she didn't hear me.

"Just one request, please," the rapper boomed from the speakers, and everyone in the room pumped their fists and chanted along to the next line: "*That all y'all suckers can choke on these!*"

The volume was lowered. "I hope to play that at my wedding someday," I said with a nervous laugh.

"What a coincidence," Sara said. "I was saving it for my father-daughter dance."

She looked down, cheeks reddening, and excused herself for the bathroom. As I refilled my drink, Ivana showed up.

"So, Sara's cute," she said, much like a mother suggesting a piece of fruit for dessert.

That word again. I considered her assessment. Sara's dishwater-brown hair was generally pulled back in a ponytail, and her face looked like a sculpture someone hadn't thought worth putting the finishing touches on, its planes and protrusions not fully defined. But when she smiled she was, I supposed, cute.

"Mmhuh," I grunted.

"Oh, you're playing it cool." She smirked. "No worries. By the way, do you have any idea if Steven's hooking up with anyone?"

"*Steven?* I doubt it."

"To both of us playing it cool, then," she toasted, bumping her beer against the rim of my cup and spilling it again.

Sara returned. Ivana gave me a knowing look as she melted back into the throng.

Two ovals of perspiration had bloomed in Sara's underarms. She noticed right after I did, noticed I'd noticed, and crossed her arms.

"Well, screw it," she said, uncrossing them. "I sweat. Big deal."

She finished her beer and I asked if she wanted another. "I was thinking about heading back, actually," she said. "But I can hang out for a little more if you want to go after this drink."

It wasn't that late yet. You might show up.

"I'll probably stick around for a while."

"Okay," she said. "See you later."

I got another drink and searched for Steven and Ivana. I didn't find them but saw a face that looked strangely familiar, as if it were the instantiation of one I'd hazily conjured up in nightmares over the years. Pug-nosed and short, he nonetheless commanded the attention of a circle of listeners. At one point he tipped his head back in amusement at something he'd himself said. Over the music

I heard a strident cackle, the sound a pterodactyl might make if it could laugh.

Scott Tupper was at Harvard.

One day in fifth grade, Jessica Waltham, one of the popular girls, passed me a note in homeroom.

"I have something to tell you at recess," she'd written. The *i* of *something* was dotted with a heart.

At the appointed time Jessica stood alone while the rest of our class frolicked on the playground. I timidly approached.

"I love you," she said, looking at her sneaker as she toed the rubber matting.

Even in those latency-phase days I understood that this was socio-romantic validation of the highest order.

"Thank you," I replied.

Neither of us spoke. Then Jessica looked over her shoulder at Scott, who had seemingly come out of nowhere, his minions in tow.

"Did he say he loves you?" he asked.

Jessica responded with a less-than-convincing nod, but that was enough to send the boys into hysterics.

I wasn't familiar with the word *entrapment*, but knew I'd been the victim of something. Nor was I aware that Scott and Jessica had recently begun "dating," whatever that meant at our age. I protested that I hadn't said I'd loved her, I'd only thanked her, but it fell on deaf ears. By the end of recess it had become gospel in the class that David F. said he was in love with Jessica.

The next day I noticed a rancid stench in my cubby as I took my winter jacket out for recess. After I zipped it up, I felt dampness on my back.

"Eww!" Scott shouted after our teacher had led the first wave of students out of the room. "David peed himself!"

His cronies howled with disgusted delight. Compounding my humiliation was that I was, in fact, an occasional bed wetter. It must have been a coincidence that he'd chosen that way to debase me, though at the time it didn't seem like one, and, feeling outed, I never reported anything to our teacher; I just wanted the incident to go away.

Those two episodes apparently quenched Scott's thirst for cruelty, as he did nothing else the rest of the year. Still, I developed a precautionary habit of sniffing my jacket before putting it on every single time, and my fears of additional torment manifested themselves in stomachaches each morning. My parents asked what was wrong, why I kept making excuses to get out of school. As much as I craved justice, I refused to tattle. Openly admitting my status as a target of bullies would authenticate it on the deepest of levels.

Scott's family moved away the next year. That he had gotten into Harvard came as a shock. He hadn't distinguished himself as a student, and I'd always assumed he would grow up into the sort of druggie who fried his brain with pot while supplying it at a suburban markup to his deep-pocketed classmates.

After refilling my cup with gin—just gin—I retreated to the opposite corner of the room, blending into the nubby white wall. Once I had enough alcohol in my system I was ready to initiate a confrontation. I advanced toward him, armed with my opening line: *Scott, it's David Federman. Remember me?*

But *I* shouldn't have had to jog *his* memory, shouldn't have had to be the one to approach; he should see me, feel guilty, and come up and beg forgiveness. I stopped before infiltrating his ring and stared at him.

We briefly made eye contact before he returned to his conversation. Not a flicker of recognition.

I was one of a few dozen forgettable boys he'd arbitrarily victimized over the years, and after a while we'd all become constituent parts of one effete, thin-wristed composite, a chorus of panicky titters preceding whatever indignity we were about to suffer.

Maybe the experience had made me more sensitive, more academically focused, and I'd been rewarded with acceptance to

Harvard; that was fine. But if the world were really fair, people like him would be punished for their loutish misdeeds, not given the same prize. The Scott Tuppers should have been banished to community college.

I stumbled home through a ginny fog, somehow fit my key into the lock, and sprawled on my bed. Drunken sleep had nearly overtaken me when I heard a sound like an army of mewling mice from Steven's room. Once I'd started to pay attention, it was too loud for me to fall asleep, so I hoisted myself up to investigate and put my ear to his door.

It wasn't rodents; it was his bouncing bedsprings.

Subatomic Steven was having sex his first week of college. And I was forced to listen to it.

I woke up for the beginning of shopping period with my first hangover and groggily dropped in on an art history lecture, The Renaissance to Impressionism, chosen purely for its convenient location. Smaller classes would have been a better way to make friends outside of the Matthews Marauders, but I hadn't applied in advance for any of the freshman seminars, which winnowed out dispassionate students by requiring an essay attesting to one's interest in the subject.

When I saw you poised to leave Annenberg at lunch, holding your tray aloft, it occurred to me that I could follow you around for the afternoon and sign up for the same classes you did.

As I took a final bite of cereal and trailed you outside, I imagined revealing to you, in the future, this moment of my taking decisive, romantic action. *Just think,* we would conjecture, *we might never have gotten together; life is so random.*

You proceeded toward the redundantly named Harvard Hall, the contours of your shoulder blades pulsing under a thin black sweater, your gait as fluid as the motion of an underwater breast-stroker. We arrived at a second-floor lecture room and you took an aisle seat. I found a free chair in the row behind, from which I had an unobstructed view of your profile.

A professor, his white hair fringing a dome that shone brilliantly under the lights, fiddled with his notes at the podium. The syllabus was distributed: From Ahab to Prufrock: Tragically Flawed Hero(in)es in American Literature, 1850–1929.

Throughout the eighty-five-minute lecture I was riveted on you and only you, the professor's voice droning like talk radio in the background. You composed notes in longhand, scribbling in your Harvard-insignia blue spiral notebook, periodically snake flicking your tongue between your lips to moisturize them before flexing the angle of your mandible. At one point you massaged your nape, precipitating a delicate flurry of dandruff that drifted onto your shoulders, becoming a constellation of stars on the night sky of your sweater.

When you tilted your head in my direction to work out a knot, I looked at my laptop screen and busily typed Professor Jonathan Samuelson's last insight, about how the whiteness of the whale in *Moby-Dick* enables it to stand for anything in the minds of both Ahab and the reader.

"Its very blankness, the colossal void it imposes on the text, reifies a central tension of post–Manifest Destiny American literature," he proclaimed with closed eyes and an upturned head, as though channeling his wisdom from above. "The twinned desires of narrative and of capitalism. The populist author entices the ravenous reader via withheld information to keep him wanting more and more, just as the free market promises additional capital to seduce the never-satisfied worker. To quote Blake, 'Those who restrain desire, do so because theirs is weak enough to be restrained . . .' Anyone know the rest? TFs?"

One of the graduate teaching fellows who had helped hand out the syllabus spoke up from the back of the room. "'And the restrainer or reason usurps its place & governs the unwilling,'" he recited behind a trim sandy beard and tortoiseshell glasses. "'And being restrain'd, it by degrees becomes passive, till it is only the shadow of desire.'"

At the end of the lecture Samuelson announced that those planning on taking the class should sign up online for one of the four graduate student–led weekly discussion sections. I had no way of knowing which one you'd be in—assuming you even remained in the course.

You slipped out ahead of me. By the time I exited the building you were traversing the Yard, your over-the-shoulder bag—its handsomely distressed leather standing out in a sea of gaudily zippered backpacks and nonprofit-logoed totes—rhythmically colliding against your hip.

I stopped and prodded at my phone when you crossed paths with one of your dining hall friends, a sharp-faced, nearly translucent girl with blond hair (Jen Pelletier, East Eighty-Seventh Street in New York; a fellow alumna of the Chapin School). You each pulled out a pack of cigarettes and lit one, in defiance of the Yard's tobacco-free policy. That was the end of your competitive running days, I surmised, not without some disappointment; I liked imagining you extricating yourself from your social circle to log hours on a chilly outdoor track, the masochistic introversion of the middle-distance runner.

And yet there was something attractive about it, a yesteryear femininity to the way you handled the cigarette. I held up my phone, zoomed in with the camera, and snapped. It caught you with a plume of smoke escaping your mouth, your lips in a perfect O. After you stamped out the butts, Jen parted with an air kiss and you continued on to Sever Hall.

Our next class was an intimate seminar. I entered the room a few students after you, and not a moment too soon, as the professor asked if I would shut the door behind me. There was only one (clearly gay) male at the oval table. Everyone looked at me as if my presence were unwelcome, a grotesque insect crawling over their lovely picnic spread.

The professor, a thirtyish woman with cat's-eye glasses and the edge of a tattoo peeking out of her jacket sleeve, reminded the class that if they were here it meant they had already signed up for the freshman seminar Gender and the Consumerist Impulse. Enrollment in the seminars was restricted to twelve. I counted thirteen students in the room.

I was sitting halfway between you and the professor, which meant I couldn't look at you—this time I was in your line of vision. As the professor lectured during a slideshow on print ads of the 1970s, I devoted all my energy to appearing attentive, knowledgeable, and *passionate*, nodding along after brief pauses as if I were mulling each comment and giving it my carefully considered imprimatur.

She opened the seminar up to discussion. A girl to my right raised her hand.

"The magnification of feminine mouths in many of the ads seems to be about isolating the one non-taboo main orifice," she said. "The female mouth takes in edible objects that substitute for the phallus."

"Absolutely," the professor said. "Male mouths are rarely eroticized. They typically function as a tool to imply speech or some other form of power."

Here was my opening, a place where I felt slightly more comfortable speaking than in an orientation session or dorm entryway. I came up with a line to simultaneously flaunt my intellect and cleverness. *Crisp*, I reminded myself. *Crisp*.

"But then you might say that the Marlboro Man ads are an example of pathetic *fallacy*," I said, referring to the campaign that had just been on-screen.

I leaned back in my chair and folded my arms, waiting for approving laughter. The silence was disconcerting.

"How so?" the professor asked.

No wonder—if she hadn't even understood the terms of the joke, there was little chance the students could.

"Pathetic fallacy is the attribution of human emotion to nature," I explained. At least her ignorance gave me another opportunity to demonstrate my knowledge, perhaps secure my spot in the seminar.

"Right," she said. "And how does that relate to the Marlboro Man?"

The room suddenly felt very warm. "Well, he's in nature, and he has a small cigarette in his mouth."

"I'm afraid I don't follow," she said. "Unless you were just making a pun on 'pathetic fallacy' and 'pathetic phallus'?"

I nodded and swallowed. The professor, stony-faced, called on another student. A disaster, worse than if I'd made an earnestly inane observation. I clammed up for the rest of the class. You didn't talk, either.

When the seminar ended I didn't follow you to your next destination. Though I was loath to let you out of my sight, I needed to speak to the professor.

"Excuse me," I said as she gathered her notes. "I didn't sign up for this seminar and I know you're at the size limit, but I'm very passionate about the subject and would be happy to write my application essay now."

I felt pinned by her glare, which seemed to convey her presumption that I, as a male whose *signifiers* (to borrow a word she used repeatedly) pointed to heterosexuality, was not here out of academic integrity but for some nefarious agenda.

"There's a wait list," she said, zipping up her bag. "If you don't get in, I'll also be teaching this next semester."

One more student would hardly upset the equilibrium; how bureaucratically compliant for someone with a tattoo and a professed interest in "nonnormative modes of intersectionality." I could only hope that one of the students would be scared off by the daunting syllabus, which culminated in a lengthy "anthropological study requiring local fieldwork."

You didn't eat lunch in Annenberg the rest of the week, foiling my designs to duplicate your course load. In addition to the English lecture, I ended up registering for the art history class I'd shopped; the massive introductory economics course; and a philosophy/psychology class, Ethical Reasoning 22: The Self and the Other.

I didn't get off the wait list for Gender and the Consumerist Impulse. The good news was that you showed up to the next lecture for Ahab to Prufrock, though we weren't slotted into the same discussion section. Our time in a shared space would be confined to Tuesday afternoons from 1:05 to 2:30 in Harvard Hall, which was just as impersonal as Annenberg. I would have to find another point of "intersectionality."

Chapter 5

I skimmed the campus events listings, found a viable candidate, and copied the link in a jaunty e-mail to Sara:

Subject: salsa? (not the condiment)

Hey, future concentrator in Latin American history, want to go to this thing tomorrow night? I warn you: I'm really good at salsa dancing. (Not really.) If you're game, I can meet you in your room and we can head over together.

A few hours later she wrote back, "I'm even better! I'll be coming from the library, so I'll meet you at the place."

Sara wasn't there when I arrived at the salsa event, hosted by a Latino students' organization in a building on Mt. Auburn Street. I dawdled by the door as the undergrads filed in and warmly greeted one another. They began to pair up and I went to the bathroom to kill time. I returned to find Sara watching from the sidelines.

"Sorry I'm late," I said. "A friend from high school called on the way here. She wouldn't stop talking."

She nodded absently, a look of trepidation on her face. "I can tell I'm going to be really bad at this," she said, eyes on the dance floor, where the couples synchronized back-and-forth steps, the more expert dancers adding spins and flourishes the execution of which were as beyond my purview as dunking a basketball.

"I didn't realize what we were getting into," I admitted. "I'm pretty sure no one would care if we sat out. Or even notice if we left."

"Maybe it's a good thing for us to experience being unseen at a Latino event," she whispered. "You know—when Latinos have to deal with being unseen more systematically every day in the U.S."

I gave her a sidelong glance to see if she was joking, but she wasn't.

To my horror, we weren't unseen. "Join us!" called out a girl who seemed to be the leader. Sara and I looked at each other self-consciously, the sixth graders jammed together by a well-meaning teacher at the school dance. With a resigned shrug she dropped her backpack to the floor and we tentatively shuffled to the outer ring of the action. I aped the stance of the men, holding my left hand up to the side. Sara took it in hers. My right hand hovered by her back without making contact, respecting an inch-wide force field. Her loose-fitting clothes—amorphous jeans, a long-sleeved shirt—stymied lecherous inspection of her figure, but from what I could tell, it carried little excess fat without being toned. A peeled potato, solid and compact. No one would ever become irritated with her in a crowd; she took up modest space.

We watched the eight-beat footsteps of the dancers subsisting on the fundamental moves. Mimicry proved challenging. Sara and I both lacked the coordination to follow the kinetic algorithm independently and were even more hopeless collaborators.

Ashamed of our ungainliness and cultural trespassing, the bovine American tourists immobilized by bulging fanny packs, I looked down at the floor, focusing on my feet. As we stepped forward at the same time, Sara's forehead struck my nose.

"Shit," I said, rubbing the spot to assess the damage.

She clapped a hand over her mouth. "I'm sorry! Are you all right?"

"Does it look broken?" I asked. "It feels broken."

"It looks okay to me." She grimaced with remorse. "I'm *so* sorry."

"I guess I'll just put some ice on it," I said. "You mind if we go home, though?"

After wrapping a few ice cubes inside a napkin at the refreshments table and holding it to my nose, we walked back to Matthews, chatting about our class schedules.

"We're doing it again," she said.

"What?"

"Small talk." She shook her head with faux sadness. "Which neither of us excels at."

"*At which* neither of us excels," I tsk-tsked. "So, have you bonded with your roommate yet?"

"Nope," she said. "You and Steven having some deep discussions?"

"Nothing beyond what you've seen in the dining hall," I said. "To be honest, you're the only one here I've really talked to in any depth."

Sara tilted her jaw down to her sternum, fighting a smile. "You, too." She looked back up. "That's what college is supposed to be for, right? Those life-changing conversations you won't have again afterward?"

"Right," I said. "So if I don't have any here, it means my life will never change. I'll always be the same person."

"Well, let's change that up," she said.

"You mean 'Let's *up* that change,'" I corrected her.

As we approached Matthews, a small branch fell on the path not far in front of us.

"If I hadn't stopped to get the ice cubes, we might've been under it when it fell," I said, looking up at the tree from which it had fallen.

"They really should cut that down. It's a negligence lawsuit waiting to happen."

"Are your parents pressuring you to become a lawyer?"

"No," I answered. "But it's the obvious option."

"That shouldn't be why you choose something so important," she said.

"Yeah," I said. "This is America, after all—I can be whatever I want. I can be a world-famous salsa dancer."

She smiled at my weak joke but didn't laugh. When we reached the fourth floor, she asked what my room number was. "There's something I want to bring you," she said.

"Is it in your room?" I asked. "I'll come get it."

We arrived at her door. You could be inside.

"Wait here—my room's a mess," Sara said, and slipped in, shutting the door before I could sneak a glimpse. She stepped out a moment later and handed me a book: *101 Idealistic Jobs That Actually Exist.*

"Hold on to it as long as you want," she told me.

I thanked her, peeked down the hall in case you were returning, and said I should get going.

"By the way," she said, "I realize that comment about Latinos' being unseen sounded pretty sanctimonious. I didn't mean to imply that you're someone who doesn't recognize his privilege."

"Not at all," I reassured her.

Sara nodded, but her face remained anxious, and she showed no indication of signing off for the night. She was waiting for something. I'd worried this might happen; I had, after all, asked a girl to go dancing, an invitation that could be interpreted as romantic. I'd hoped she wouldn't regard it as anything more than an overture of friendship, the kind that evolved into hanging out in her room and, inevitably, meeting her roommate.

I had already run a cost-benefit analysis of a sexual relationship with Sara. Not only would it take me off the market, but my association with her could diminish my standing in your eyes. Yet it also meant I'd be around you much more than I would if we were Platonic; as I was now learning, she wasn't even letting me *see* her room. And it was college. These things didn't last forever.

Despite my certainty that a kiss would be reciprocated, the prospect of instigating it remained unduly terrifying; like a trust-your-new-summer-camp-buddies fall backward, it went against every instinct of self-preservation. No one was around, but it felt to me as if the whole campus, my high school, even my parents and sisters, were watching. If I didn't do it, I'd be unmanned in front of them, the boy who, after eighteen years, had finally found a girl willing to kiss him—and he couldn't even go through with it.

I closed my eyes and, impelled more by fear than desire, made the trust fall forward. Our lips touched and soon yielded to tongues, which grappled like junior-varsity wrestlers trying to impress the coach with their hustle. I was too conscious that I was having a legitimate sexual experience to bask mindlessly in the sensory pleasures. Nonetheless, I achieved an erection that was deftly hidden by *101 Idealistic Jobs That Actually Exist*.

Bizarre verb, *achieved*, as if to remind you of the possibility of failure and all its attendant disgrace.

Chapter 6

And so began a courtship. Since parties weren't Sara's thing, we gorged on the menu of on-campus activities: film screenings, plays, world-music concerts, and guest speakers. Afterward she was raring to discuss whatever we'd seen. I tried to engage for her sake, but if I wasn't being tested on the subject matter, it was hard for me to care. During our study dates in Lamont Library, she read every word assigned to her, meticulously underlined and highlighted and marginalia'd, sought out competing perspectives, researched auxiliary material. An academic mule, if one motivated by genuine curiosity.

All our rendezvous were in public. Whenever I suggested doing something that would get me into Sara's room, I was frustrated by her goaltender's knack for deflecting me. "I'm kind of burned out on the library," I texted one night. "I'd say we could study here but Steven has been popping out to practice magic tricks on me all day. Maybe your room?" (A lie; Steven was a reactor core of interpersonal fuel, joining a raft of clubs, picking up new friends like a lint roller, and entering into a relationship with Ivana that entailed incessant fondling and pet names. Stevie-bean spent most nights in Ivana-suck-your-blood's room, so I couldn't really complain, though he indulged in one instance of grating boastfulness, requesting that a picture of himself and his parents reside on my bookcase, not his. "Why?" I asked. "It's weird to feel like they're staring at me when Ivana's in there," he said with put-on embarrassment. "You know how it is.")

"Let's go to Starbucks!" Sara replied.

Our physical contact was restricted to PG make-out sessions by the lawsuit tree near Matthews, an awkward location, since we couldn't part immediately after kissing. Instead, we had to walk another few dozen paces to our dorm, go upstairs together, and, at the fourth floor, she would wave like a friendly neighbor before continuing her ascent to your castle in the faraway kingdom of 505, where you remained out of my sight—though very much on my mind.

Location was also a problem the next two Prufrock classes, when you snuck in late and chose seats out of my field of vision. You were the whole reason I was taking the class—and dating your roommate—but we might as well have been at different schools.

One evening Sara and I attended a lecture by a visiting economist with the elaborate title "Antisocial Mobility: The Impossible Transcendence of Previously Permeable Socioeconomic Borders." I daydreamed about you through the whole talk, but snapped to attention when, as we shambled out of the auditorium, Sara at last asked if I wanted to study in her room.

On the way back to Matthews, the excitement leavening my step had little to do with the sexual promise of what lay in store. In fact, while I wasn't about to reject the leap forward we were about to take—maybe even hurdling over all the preliminary obstacles straight to the final one—I couldn't help feeling a little disappointed that Sara might be my first.

"Those stats he brought up were scary, about how the situation you're born into more than ever determines your economic fate," Sara said as we walked back.

"Mmm," I said.

"I was getting really depressed listening to him, but at the end, in a weird way, I started thinking all his pessimism about America is actually almost optimistic, because he's also basically saying, 'If we made this, it means we can unmake it.' And the real travesty isn't what's already happened, but continuing to let it happen and resigning ourselves to it."

"Yeah," I said. "Good point."

Your door was closed. Sara's room was neat, contrary to her previous claims, and modestly appointed. Around her desk were framed photographs of her family: the diffident younger sister who closely resembled her; the gregarious older brother who was a blunt-featured male version; the jolly, ursine father whose genes had been lost in transmission; the graying, bifocaled mother into whom Sara would someday evolve.

Sara sat on her bed, knees propping up *Anti-Imperialist Marxism in Latin America*. I stationed myself at her desk and began reading *The Scarlet Letter*.

"You can sit here, you know," she told me a few minutes later, patting the mattress. I moved over, leaving enough space for a phantom body between the two of us and resting against the cool wall that separated her room from yours.

"At least she's quiet," I whispered, pointing toward your door. "Nothing worse than a noisy roommate."

"I doubt she's home," Sara said. As she read, her forehead squinched around a central point and the tip of her tongue explored the corner of her mouth, an expression of concentration I would come to know well. After a while she announced she was tired and asked if I wanted to go to bed.

"Okay," I said, unsure if this was an invitation or a tactful request to leave.

"I'll go brush my teeth and change," she said.

She left for the bathroom, carrying her toiletries kit, a pair of gray athletic shorts, and an oversized shirt that said RAISE OHIO'S MINIMUM WAGE NOW! I stayed put, alone in the room, desperately waiting for your entrance.

A few minutes later I heard a key in the door. Too nervous to look up, I kept my eyes on the book, pretending to read, but then the door opened and Sara's voice was muttering, "People waste so much water here." I waited for her to extinguish the light before removing my jeans. My shirt I kept on; if she was going to remain clothed, so was I. My physique, I knew, wasn't much to look at, but as a purely tactile experience in the dark, it would be unobjectionable.

I climbed in under the pink flannel sheets, a reprieve from my own scratchy, cotton/poly-blend bedding (which, if I ever got you into it, I would claim was my backup, and then blow my entire semester's petty cash on a high-thread-count upgrade). Sara turned on a white-noise machine. "You mind?" she asked. "It's kind of loud, but I need it to fall asleep."

We lay on our backs on the narrow mattress, our shoulders but nothing else touching, her body an environmentally friendly space heater. The white-noise machine was, indeed, loud; I would never hear anything in your room over it. As it thrummed, our stomachs produced gurgly video game sounds. Neither of us was making a move, two disoriented and jet-lagged travelers stepping off a plane in a foreign country, unsure if we had to go first to customs or the baggage claim.

Then, imagining the warmth next to me was radiating from you, I grew hard and found myself, almost without any conscious self-direction, turning to kiss Sara. We continued for several minutes in an uncomfortable, torqued position until I rotated on top of her, hoping you'd come in, inconsiderately flip the switch, and view me in a newly sexual light.

I reached for the hem of her shirt. (Oh, Ohio's minimum-wage

movement, if only you knew how your lofty ideals would someday be corrupted.) We were in college, far from watchful parents.
It might actually happen. I could reply to Daniel Hallman's stupid
message.

Her fingers interlaced with mine with a cheerful squeeze, as
if hand-holding were what I was really after. I brought my other
hand down and was likewise rejected. Now all four were clasped
as I bodysurfed on top of her with our legs braided together, a two-
headed octopus in coitus interceptus.

I took the double hint and lifted our tentacles out of harm's way.
Without any demarcating biological event, it was up to one of us to
call a ceasefire. I let my kissing subside and parallel parked myself
on the wall side of the bed. We spoke only about practical matters: if
I wanted water, what time to set the alarm on her phone.

"Is your roommate going to wake us up?" I asked.

"No," Sara said. "If she comes home, she knows not to turn on
the lights anymore."

"*If* she comes home? Where would she be?"

"You do the math," she said.

We spooned amateurishly, my body acclimating to the alien
sensation of sustained contact with someone else's, my forearm
losing circulation under her upper back, my other arm unsure
what to do with itself, until I retracted both and flipped over.
Sara's breathing slowed to sleeping pace as I listened for any
sound of the door opening, pondering your whereabouts, sorting
through the male regulars at your Annenberg table: the one with
landscaped stubble (Andy Tweedy), the black guy who favored
scarves (Christopher Banks), the rumored Italian baron (Marco
Lazzarini).

I stayed awake until dawn pressed through the window shade,
and woke up when Sara's phone tinkled at eight and she took a birth
control pill. "To regulate my period," she explained awkwardly. No
signs of your wee-hours entrance, if there'd been one.

A few nights later, after a documentary about migrant laborers in the Southwest, we went back to her room again. Sara talked about how she wanted to see more documentaries, how easy it was to get into an academic bubble here and forget how unjust the world was.

"Well," I said, "in the long run we're all dead."

She squinted at me. "So it's all right if there are inequalities now, because eventually we're all dead anyway?"

I smoothed out her comforter with my hand.

"That's a pretty cynical sentiment," she said. "There are a lot of people whose lives are almost exclusively hardship. Just because we all *die* at the end doesn't make it even."

"I was only trying to lighten the mood," I said.

"I know." She reached for her copy of *Anti-Imperialist Marxism in Latin America* and handed it to me. "But check this out when you get a chance." She left for ablutions in the bathroom.

What I wanted was impossible; even this starter relationship was in danger of collapse. How foolishly optimistic to think it might somehow lead to you. When Sara came back I'd tell her that we'd made a mistake and should go back to being friends before anyone got hurt.

As if you'd heard my doubts and were telling me not to surrender, that nothing worthwhile was ever acquired without a struggle, the door was unlocked from the hallway. You looked at me with the vague recognition one has for a stranger on the same daily bus commute and walked toward your room.

"Aren't you in Prufrock?" I asked, hoping to salvage the moment.

"Yeah."

"Me, too. I'm David."

"Nice to meet you," you said as you opened your door, acknowledging there was no need to add your name—I'd have seen it on the sign outside, but I'd have known it anyway, much as I imagine celebrities don't have to introduce themselves. And we'd met before, of course, but your error comforted me: our doorway encounter had been so undistinguished that I preferred it be stricken from the record.

Sara returned. "Your roommate's back," I said softly while fake reading her book about the unjustness of the world.

She lowered her voice. "Aren't we lucky."

I grinned in bogus conspiracy. She had some e-mails to respond to and asked if I minded if she took care of them before bed. "Happy to wait," I said.

I didn't have to wait long. You emerged from your room in a white silk bathrobe and flip-flops, a towel over your shoulder and a toiletries basket by your side. My eyes flew a brief reconnaissance mission over the terrain of your calves: still bronzed, the elevated plateaus of muscle sloping down defined cliffs to the lower planes of your Achilles tendons. Elegant, lean feet, callused heels; it looked like you'd spent a lot of time barefoot in the summer. Other guys, the philistines who chugged domestic light beer, might have salivated over the body parts your robe concealed, but I was a connoisseur of your peripheral qualities, an oenophile who sussed out your fruity bouquets and spicy notes.

"Hey," you said to Sara on your way out.

"Hey," Sara said, eyes on her laptop screen.

The next twenty minutes felt like days, my imagination rioting with you in the shower. You came back enrobed and glistening, your hair wrapped in the towel. The robe was monogrammed with a stitched, proud wound of *VMW* over your heart. As you opened the door to your room, an air current caught the tip of the lightweight belt, which fluttered up as if of its own accord.

A hair dryer rumbled in your room. Going out to parts unknown. Worse, you knew precisely what I was doing: tragically staring at a Marxist tome with your bookish roommate. I'd given myself more opportunity for surveillance of you, but it meant you were now privy to my own humdrum existence.

"Night," you said as you left.

Sara nodded in your direction. "See ya," I called to your back.

Sara asked if I was ready for bed. I put down the book, waited for her to turn off the lights, and stripped to my boxers and T-shirt.

Once again we lay side by side until, eventually, I kissed and mounted her. It looked like it was going to be the same restrained tussle as before, but tonight I was more driven. I thought of you—in your robe, in the shower—as I rammed against Sara's dreary gray shorts. This time I succeeded in lifting the RAISE OHIO'S MINIMUM WAGE NOW! shirt. Her breasts were, to my untrained cupping, perfectly adequate. I pulled off my shirt, hoping my own nudity would induce her to shed additional layers. It didn't.

"Hold on," Sara said. She fumbled over her bedside table and her hand came back with a plastic pump dispenser she pressed into mine. "You can use this."

In the dark, I didn't know what it was or what its utility would be.

"It's lotion," she clarified. "Don't guys do that? On themselves?"

I took off my boxers and applied the lotion to my erection as I straddled her lower body. With my left hand on her breast, my right took care of myself. I'd never done this in the presence of anyone, but it felt oddly natural.

Then she did something that surprised me: she rubbed under her shorts, her eyes shut, her breaths quickening. As she continued to worry her clitoris, I stayed silent until my denouement, when I startled myself with a squelched grunt. The seed that had been buried in innumerable shrouds of Kleenex now, for once, ended up on another human being.

Sara kept going until her own climax, a small affair that seized up her core muscles before releasing them like a bout of pleasurable indigestion. She reached on top of her bedside table for the white T-shirt she'd worn that day and mopped up her stomach and rib cage. Dropping it on the floor, she put her RAISE OHIO'S MINIMUM WAGE NOW! shirt back on, then curled her back against my chest. I slung an arm around her.

"Confession," she said. "I've never done that before."

I didn't say anything, just breathed on her neck.

"Have you?" she asked.

"Mmhuh," I said.

Her heartbeat was palpable to my cradling arm. "Well," she said, "I hope you're not intimidated by my extensive erotic record."

A humble, self-deprecating remark that, a couple of weeks earlier, would have made me banter back with wordplay, maybe compel me to recant my statement and tell her the truth. But now, after I'd captured you pre- and post-shower, Sara's inexperience only reminded me that we were two virgins and that you were adventuring elsewhere on campus. People like *you* didn't mutually masturbate—you had sex. No, even that was putting too chaste a spin on it. You fucked.

Citore drocer, I thought.

"That's all right," I said, offering neither any real assurance nor a lighthearted follow-up to put her at ease. My arm remained around her, but it suddenly felt like it wasn't mine anymore, a prosthetic limb.

Another silence as her wheels turned for the phrasing of her next question. "Did you have a girlfriend in high school?"

"Heidi," I answered.

"When were you together?"

"Tenth grade on."

"When'd you break up?"

"This summer," I said. "She wanted to stay together for college. I didn't."

Sara processed that revelation for some time. "What was she like?"

"She was nice."

"Was she pretty?"

"Well, she was the lead in most plays. I guess that says something."

"Who's prettier, me or her?" Sara asked, then quickly laughed. "Just kidding."

I yawned loudly. "I'm actually kind of tired. Mind if we go to sleep?"

"Of course," she said.

As I dozed off to the white-noise machine, I stroked Sara's arm, mentally elongating it until it reached your lithe proportions.

The one way to guarantee I sat by you in Prufrock would be to wait for you to enter the room first, tricky to engineer, since you were consistently late to class. The next Tuesday I stood outside the door in Harvard Hall, pecking at my phone. As the students trickled in and you still hadn't shown, I grew anxious; I'd yet to be tardy for any classes, and though they didn't take attendance at the lectures, I didn't want to blemish my self-monitored perfect record.

When I heard, through the door, Samuelson begin his lecture, I gave myself a deadline: three more minutes.

Five minutes later I was about to go in, when I heard footsteps coming up the stairs. I stole a look down the hallway to confirm it was you, pocketed my phone with the certitude of someone finished with his important business, and looked up.

"Hey," I said.

You nodded. There was now, at least, instant facial identification.

I opened the door for you. You went to the nearest empty seat. It didn't look strange when I sat in the one next to it; we'd entered the room together and these were the easiest-to-reach places.

I would be sitting within a foot of you for eighty minutes. There was no chance I could follow Samuelson's winding disquisition on *The Portrait of a Lady* and *Daisy Miller*.

My peripheral vision was limited to your left hand, its blue rivers of veins faintly flowing under smooth skin, its piano-player fingers, its pale pink nails and their small white suns cresting over the curved horizon. I could absorb more comprehensively your scent, whose intimations that I'd nosed before now blanketed me: an amalgam of your shampoo and lavender perfume, a hint of cigarettes and whatever natural aroma you exuded. If I could inhale it continuously, eternally, without ever breathing out, I would.

Samuelson riffled through papers on his lectern as he prattled on. "One of you wrote an essay this week that nicely dovetails with that point. Let me just find it . . ."

We overestimate destiny's role in our lives, selectively applying it to favorable outcomes; think of all the times when you *didn't* run into your long-lost friend in the street, when you *didn't* just catch a bus, when you *didn't* get placed in a dorm with Veronica Morgan Wells. Or, more starkly, of all the good things that never happened to you because you weren't born as someone else with a better life. But the law of averages—which, when advantageous to us, we prefer to call fate, when disadvantageous we decry as bad luck, and when neutral we ignore—will occasionally smile upon us when we most need it.

Samuelson located the correct paper. "David Federman argued that, quote, 'perhaps the peg-leg-as-primal-wound is intended to throw the reader off the scent with a facile psychological misreading, and Melville's underlying point is that Ahab is simply a susceptible participant in an economic system designed for manic, unslakable ambition. The real primal wound is not his missing leg; it is America.'"

I hadn't even known Samuelson *read* the student essays; my section leader must have been so taken with my writing that she'd pressed it on him. It was thrilling to hear those sentences preached to the entire room, especially the final clause, intoned with the halting majesty of a presidential peroration or the voice-over in a domestic car commercial. Rendering the experience even more exhilarating: you, in an orchestra seat to witness my glory.

"David, are you here?" Samuelson asked, peering out into the crowd, since he didn't know who I was.

Everyone looked around for the mystery writer. I raised my hand slowly, as if reluctant to take credit.

I savored your surprise next to me: you didn't know who David Federman was, either; might not have even remembered my first name and certainly didn't know my last. You wouldn't forget it now.

"It's a compelling idea—I'd love to discuss it further," Samuelson said to me. "Sign up for office hours."

He dismissed us. My body, to others, remained earthbound, but I was in a crow's nest high above them. And good luck, let alone destiny, had nothing to do with it. No; years of solitude, hours spent reading when others were going to birthday parties and sleepovers and keggers, had all built up to Professor Samuelson's public acclamation for an essay I'd tossed off in a single sitting. I imagined him inviting me to guest lecture an upcoming class, whatever topic I liked; he just wanted the other students to be inspired by my example, and you would sit in the front row, transcribing every word, marveling at my harpoon-sharp mind.

I stood up poker-faced, the star running back who no longer needs to spike the football in the end zone to celebrate his victories.

"Nice work," you said as we filed out.

"Oh, thanks," I said. "What did you write about?"

"I got an extension till tomorrow. I haven't started yet."

We stepped out into the honeyed light of a New England autumn afternoon. Students were starting to wear scarves. The air was spiced with the first fallen leaves. A breeze trembled a nearby oak, showering the pavement with acorns.

I walked with purpose in the direction of Sever, knowing you were heading there for Gender and the Consumerist Impulse.

"Which book are you writing about?" I asked.

"No idea," you said. "I'm fucked."

You didn't mind cursing with me, cursing with a sexual term, with a sexual term that, as a sentence, could also suggest an explicit action.

"What about *Moby-Dick*?"

"Mm," you said, unimpressed. "Seven-hundred-page books by dead white men aren't exactly my bag."

"Yeah, I know." I chuckled. "What's interested you most so far?"

"I liked *Daisy Miller*."

We were approaching Sever; I was running out of time, and this wasn't a dialogue I could easily continue in Sara's room.

I stopped walking. "I have to be somewhere," I said—I had nowhere to be, nothing to do, all I wanted was to continue even this seemingly mundane conversation forever—"but if you're having trouble, I'd be happy to help you come up with a topic later."

Your eyes blinked at me once, as if you were taking my measurements for something. Your irises were three distinct hues: a fine outer ring of grayish blue like an overcast ocean sky that yielded to springtime emerald before melting into a striated core the color of bourbon. I couldn't meet them for more than a second or two.

"How about Lamont at nine?" you asked.

Sara spent half her nights there. But Widener Library closed at ten, and there was no good alternative, other than my room, which I didn't have the temerity to suggest.

"Works for me," I said.

Chapter 7

After getting a sandwich at Au Bon Pain, I holed up in my room to reread *Daisy Miller* along with the secondary critical texts Samuelson had assigned. I graffitied the pages with notes for once, just like Sara did.

I texted her that I'd be forgoing dinner to work on an essay for my art history class. "Good luck! I'm feeling a cold coming on ☹," she wrote back. She was perpetually afflicted with some mild ailment, a sniffle or cough or epidermal reaction. A plastic kit in her room housed a pharmacy of purple syrups, nasal sprays, blister-pack tablets. The sight of her blowing her nose or swallowing an anti-diarrheal pill always made me consider how poorly she would fare if she'd been born in another time, weeded out by natural selection. Her sneezes, induced by a plethora of allergens, came in quadrupled, body-quaking blasts that pierced the eardrum and embarrassed me by association. You must have heard them through the door.

"Aww, feel better! ☺," I replied.

As I left Matthews at 8:40 to arrive at Lamont early, I heard my name.

"Where are you going?" Sara's voice echoed in the entryway. I looked back as she sped downstairs to catch me, tissue in hand, her nostrils ruddy and chapped.

"To work on my essay. What about you?"

"CVS." She honked into the tissue, examining the deposit before folding it up. "I ran out of zinc lozenges."

"That sucks," I said, pushing the door open.

"Pun *int*ended," she chirped. "Want to come with me?"

A detour to CVS would set me back ten minutes, maybe more. If there were no delays and I hurried, I would just make it to Lamont by nine.

"I should really get going on this essay," I said.

"Please?" She pouted. "I'm going out of my mind—I haven't talked to a single person today."

The demerits for denying her this small courtesy would not be worth it in the long run. This is what chivalrous boyfriends did, and that's what I was becoming: a boyfriend who held doors, who insisted upon paying, who told her she looked nice before she went out—grooming myself for the day I could extend this behavior to you.

"Okay, let's go." I clucked my tongue sympathetically. "Poor, sick Sara."

Wandering the fluorescent aisles of CVS in search of zinc, Sara recapped the highlights of her most recent conversation with her grandmother. I pulled my phone a few inches out of my pocket: 8:48. Upon locating the medication, Sara studied the ingredient lists on two different packages, the now-familiar dimple forming on her forehead.

"The question is, should I get the *generic* brand or the real kind?" she asked herself.

I pictured you standing outside Lamont, wondering where that loser from your class could be, who did he think he was.

"They're the same exact ingredients, but I always feel like the real one is better," she reasoned.

"Get the real one, then."

She struggled to fit the small hole at the top of the generic bag over its metal peg. "I'll do it," I said, taking it from her and hanging it up myself.

"Wait." She shook her head. "This is silly. They're the same, and the generic is cheaper."

"Fine." I pulled it back off the peg. "I'll buy it for you," I offered, to expedite the process, as I headed toward the checkout. An elderly woman monopolized the only cashier, paying with exact change, shakily counting aloud her nickels and pennies.

"Do you want to donate a dollar to pediatric cancer research?" the cashier asked when I paid.

"No," I said. "And I don't need a receipt."

"What's the hurry?" Sara asked as I raced outside.

"I'm eager to get back to this essay."

"A few minutes isn't going to kill your motivation," she said.

The peremptory orange hand of the pedestrian signal had just lit up and a few cars were approaching from down Mass Ave.

"You're right," I said, putting my own hand on her lower back, resisting the urge to push her more forcefully. "Let's cross."

I guided her across the street. We had to break into a trot halfway to avoid being struck. It gave me a small rush.

"David!" Sara said when we made it to the curb. "We almost got hit!"

"We were fine," I said.

We drew up to Matthews at two minutes to nine. If you were leaving from there at an appropriate time, you might see us and, thinking it was no big deal, tell Sara what we were up to.

"Feel better," I said. "I'll talk to you tomorrow."

"I'll walk you over. Lamont, right?"

Widener closed in an hour, which she knew, so I couldn't

reasonably pretend I was going there and then wait until she left. "You don't need to walk me."

"I don't mind."

"You really shouldn't be out in the cold if you're sick."

The entryway door opened and my throat closed. But it was just a student from China I'd seen around the dorm.

"You know that's a myth," said Sara. "It's because people are inside more during cold weather that germs spread. So, really, I should *avoid* the indoors."

"Look, I don't want to catch your cold," I said, more brusquely than I'd intended. "Sorry, I didn't mean to snap. But I'm afraid of getting sick when I have a big night ahead of me."

"No, I get it," she said.

"Get some sleep," I told her, and leaned down to give her a peck on the top of her head. Her hair felt like crunchy grass on my lips.

You were neither outside nor in the lobby when I arrived at the library at 9:05. I sat on the front steps, afraid you'd impatiently left, forgotten, or blown it off.

With each passing minute I grew more convinced you'd shown up and departed when I was ensnared at CVS. Your paper was due tomorrow; I wouldn't get another opportunity to work with you like this. I should never have agreed to go with Sara.

You showed up nearly half past the hour.

"Sorry," you greeted me, not looking all that apologetic. I suppose this was one of the privileges of being who you were: you didn't have to care, because you knew I, or whoever was waiting, would be overjoyed simply to have an audience with you. Your cheeks were flushed from the cold and your hair was in slight disarray, like you'd recently woken up.

"No problem, I just got here." I scrambled to my feet and opened the door for you.

I proposed we go to the less crowded second floor. In the event of a surprise visit from Sara we would be harder to find. If she did somehow see us, I would later tell her you and I ran into each other and decided to work together. The counterintuitive benefit of your preternatural beauty was that our meeting would prompt no suspicion, as it might have with someone closer to my weight class.

We located an empty table in a secluded nook. You opened your laptop. My heart was thumping too fast. I tried to think of our meeting as a casual tutoring session and nothing more.

"So," I said, taking out my copy of the James, "*Daisy Miller*. What appeals to you about it?"

"What Samuelson was talking about today was sort of interesting," you answered. "The use of the male gaze."

"The Mulvey essay," I said encouragingly, and ventured a joke. "It's great how much social progress the male gays have made lately. Pun *int*ended."

It took you a moment to separate the homophones. Then you let out a puff of air by way of laughter. It wasn't the gag of the century, but it had done the trick.

"Which part of Mulvey's argument resonated with you?"

"To be honest," you said, "I read it, but I didn't really understand it."

"So, in film, the camera assumes the role of the scopophilic male eye," I explained. "It objectifies the passive female characters, leering at their physicality, and the audience internalizes that viewpoint."

"Scopo-what?"

"Scopo*philic*. It means deriving pleasure from looking, especially at erotic objects, sometimes to substitute for participation."

"Okay," you said. "I think I have an idea for the paper. Do you mind sticking around while I write the beginning, to see if I'm on the right track?"

"Of course."

Ten minutes later you proudly showed me what you had produced on the screen.

In the novel "Daisy Miller" by Henry James the character Win-
terbourne is scopafilic when he looks at Daisy. He derives pleasure from looking at her beauty to substitute for participating in
talking to her.

It wasn't just seven-hundred-page novels by dead white men;
literary criticism didn't seem to be your bag, either. But you were
clever in other ways, I could tell (*veritas*), which must have been
reflected in your Harvard application.

"Hmm," I said. "You've got some good ideas here. I think you
might be able to dig a little deeper, though."

You closed your eyes, rolled your neck back, and let out an audi-
ble sigh in anticipation of the hours of exertion ahead.

"I don't know how I'm going to do this in one night." Your eyes
opened and targeted me expectantly, hopefully. "Do you have anywhere to be? Would you be able to hang out and help me with the rest?"

I could have told you then that it was a great start and wished
you well, sat away from you in class, broken up with Sara to decap-
itate temptation, and quit while I was ahead. It's what high school
David, who considered it a daredevil maneuver to eject a USB connection before the computer informed me it was safe, would have
levelheadedly advised.

"I could give you a hand," I said.

"Thank you," you said. "That's really nice of you."

"Not at all." This was the occasion to prove my intellectual value
to you, to make myself indispensable. And, really, this wasn't any
different from one person helping another with a math problem set.

I turned the laptop back to you.

"So, quick tip, titles of books are italicized, not put in quotes," I
said. "And it's actually a novella, not a novel."

You keyed in the changes. "I wish I wasn't such a slow typer. This
is going to take forever."

"Here, want me to type?" I asked.

"That'd be great," you said, rotating the screen around again.

"Sometimes I like to begin by citing a single piece of evidence from the text to support my thesis," I said. "Is there anything we can bring up here, a plot event or a line?"

"I don't know."

"Well, how about the fact that the original title is *Daisy Miller: A Study*. What do you think of when you hear the words 'a study'?"

"A painting?"

"Good. So how might that connect to your thesis?"

You shrugged.

"Maybe something to do with scopophilia?" I asked.

"I should get us some coffee," you said. "It sounds like we're going to be here awhile. I'll be right back—you can keep working."

Typing your essay with you across the table was one thing; ventriloquizing you in your absence was another. Every alarm in my suburban soul was clanging, warning of violations of the honor code, academic execution at the hands of the Administrative Board, my irreversible migration into an ethical wasteland. What would Mrs. Rice say? What if Professor Samuelson found out that his best student was helping someone *cheat*?

I deleted your tenth-grade paragraph and began writing in Harvard-level prose.

"How's it coming along?" you asked, setting down a cup of coffee for me. I read aloud the rewritten thesis:

> The relationships in *Daisy Miller: A Study* (its original title) are formed by observation—by "study"—and not by conversation. The heroine captivates the scopophilic Winterbourne because he can only surmise as to the mystery of the "ambiguity of Daisy's behavior" beneath her deceptive, problematizing pulchritude.

"'Pulchritude'?" you asked.

"Beauty."

You nodded. "Nice writing," you said, as if you were realizing only now that you'd picked the perfect person to help you with your essay.

I raised my eyebrows modestly and plowed through the rest of it, reciting each paragraph for your approval before proceeding. In between typing sprees, my eyes glued to the screen as if lost in lyrical thought, I occasionally asked harmless questions, some of which I already knew the answers to, affecting a tone of absentminded indifference.

"So where are you from?"

"The city."

"New York?"

Park Avenue. The Chapin School. Veronica Morgan Wells.

"Uh-huh."

"Where'd you go to high school?"

"Chapin. Why, are you from New York?"

"No, but I know some people from there," I said.

"How about you?"

After being forced to name my high school and home state, I asked if you had any siblings.

"Nope," you said, confirming my earlier research, and rerouted the query to me.

We continued in this fashion: I'd ask you a question that you'd answer with a one-word reply before volleying it back. Even if I wasn't learning additional information about you, it was still going better than anything I could have planned; the simple act of sitting together for so long was enabling us to develop something of a rapport. But then around midnight I asked how you were liking Harvard so far.

"Have you ever noticed everyone not here always asks how you like *Harvard*?" you reflected. "Not 'How do you like college?' or 'How do you like school?' or 'How's your freshman year going?' but 'How do you like *Harvard*?' like it's some kind of celebrity. And then the flip side is that Harvard students are terrified to tell other people where they go to school, except they actually love it when it comes up."

"Yeah," I said, though no one other than my mother had reached out to ask me and I hadn't had a chance to "drop the H-bomb," as they called it, with anyone besides high school classmates before graduation. "Well, how are you liking your four-year institution of higher learning?"

"I absolutely love every precious moment," you said with a sarcastic edge. "Don't you?"

I wasn't sure how to answer. You could snarkily lead on that not everything met your standards, but if I said as much, I'd sound like a self-pitying Eeyore; it would be more attractive to make my life here seem like an endless parade of indulgent frivolities so far. Then again, you were opening up to me, intimating that you were disenchanted. You might recognize what we had in common if I took the risk and told the truth about my experience, that I felt out of place even at Harvard, human interactions put an immense strain on me, I was also somewhat of a loner at heart.

"So far so good," I said.

"Hey, mind if I do some reading?" you asked, taking out the course pack for Gender and the Consumerist Impulse.

Sometimes I wonder if, having the ability to time travel back to certain moments in which our fear or impulsiveness got the best of us and resulted in an unsatisfying outcome, we would actually alter our behavior knowing what we know now, or if we would end up repeating exactly what we did the first time, surrendering to those elemental directives, incapable of deviating from some preordained essence of our character.

"Be my guest," I said, and typed up a flurry as if I'd just had a brainstorm, worried you might say you were ready to go to bed and I'd forfeit you altogether.

"How about this?" I read from the new paragraph: " 'Daisy can also be viewed as a—' "

"I trust your judgment," you said. "You don't have to ask my permission."

A few minutes later you left for the bathroom. I had unsupervised access to your computer. After peeping around the corner to ensure you weren't coming back early, I clicked on your web browser and visited Harvard's webmail page, but you weren't signed in.

I returned to Word, where, I realized, I could read the documents you'd recently opened without much trouble. That was my brand of espionage: rummaging through the academic papers of the object of my desire.

The file menu displayed the names of four documents: the *Daisy Miller* paper we (I) were currently working on; "de beauvoir response" (you'd read *The Second Sex* that week for Gender and the Consumerist Impulse, whose syllabus I had saved and been keeping track of); "darwin - worksheet 4," apparently for the class on evolution I was kicking myself for not shopping; and one mysteriously labeled "log."

A code name for your journal? An acronym for a list of guys you were dating? A poem about chopped wood?

I opened it. All it contained was a short list of dates, starting at 10/1 and ending the day before:

10/1: $200 dinner at Menton; $35 cab fare to/from—i
10/2: watched college football; $80 on food/drink—c
10/3: bought tampons at CVS ($4)—f
10/4: N/A

It was a confusing budget; I could see how an expensive dinner would rate a mention, but not why buying tampons would. And the codes of *i*, *c*, and *f* were even more perplexing.

You returned to your seat and startled me.

"Didn't mean to scare you," you said.

"You didn't," I said, closing "log" and clicking again on the *Daisy*

Miller essay so it appeared to be the last opened document. "I forgot to put in your TF's name at the top. What is it?"

"Tom," you said. "Tom Burkhart." That was the grad student who had supplied the Blake quotation the first class, and since then, whenever Samuelson interrupted his lecture to invite the four teaching fellows to show off their familiarity with an esoteric line of poetry, he routinely spoke it in as offhand a tone as if stating the day of the week, so much so that Samuelson had begun asking Tom directly. (I always felt a prick of transitive rejection when my own TF, a dowdy woman named Harriet, stayed quiet.)

I typed in your first name, too, but before adding "Wells" I asked, "And your last name?"

You told me. "Acinorev sllew," I said after I'd transcribed it.

"What?"

"That's your name backward," I said. "Only, if you wanted to make it readable in a mirror, it'd be 'sllew acinorev.' And you'd have to print the words in reverse."

You weren't like those baseball players; I expected you to probe, then I'd explain its origins and my unique and rather intriguing college essay, you'd tell me you, too, felt like you had always seen the world differently from everyone else, though you couldn't conceive of being able to flip words around in your mind fluently, how exactly do you do that?

But "Ah" was all you said.

The library was nearly deserted by the time I finished the paper. We walked through the Yard in the silence of the small hours, under a black canvas perforated by a few dim pinholes, a diorama with us as the only figurines.

When you discovered that Matthews was also my destination, you asked, "You're seeing Sara now?"

"No, I live here, too."

"Oh," you said with a small note of surprise.

"This is me," I said when we reached the fourth floor.

You continued on up. "Thanks for your help."

"Anytime," I called out. "I'm always available to rescue a damsel in distress."

You paused midflight and looked down at me, a weird grin on your face.

"Good night, Divad," you said, and kept walking.

For a moment I thought you'd somehow gotten my name, my easiest of names, wrong, but then I realized you were saying it backward. My paranoia was unwarranted—you'd been impressed with my idiosyncratic talent, after all.

I climbed into bed, though I wasn't remotely tired; your "Divad" had revived my endorphins. Lying under the sheets, I tried reading in preparation for my meeting with Samuelson but couldn't concentrate. This *was* going to be the best year of my life, a Technicolor romp after so many dunnish slogs. I pulled up my window shade and watched the stars fade into the lightening sky, imagining us speaking whole sentences to each other in my reversed preadolescent tongue, an exclusive mode of communication. *Veronica and David,* people would say, *those two have their own language—they're the only ones who understand each other.*

Chapter 8

My finger hovered over my laptop's touch pad with the grave deliberation associated with launching a nuclear strike. It had been thirty-six hours since our evening at Lamont—more than enough time for a friend request on Facebook to seem an afterthought. We were both at Harvard, we lived in the same dorm, we'd "studied" together; this was a perfectly ordinary next step. After you accepted, I'd be able to view your trove of photos and status updates, maybe learn something that would help me win you over—similar tactics had panned out in a number of romantic comedies I'd seen—or at least discover where you were spending your nights.

I clicked.

I didn't use the site myself except for voyeurism. I was friends with my high school and Matthews confederacies, a smattering of relatives, and the people who sluttishly befriend everyone on it. To avoid advertising the paucity of my social connections, I had hidden my list of friends and prohibited anyone from posting on my wall.

Before arriving at Harvard, I'd hoped I would acquire such a bounty of comrades here that I could make my social media presence more transparent, perhaps even add the popular kids from Hobart High to show them how far I'd come. Yet for now I wasn't eager to be seen in pictures with the Matthews Marauders nor to affirm my relationship with Sara, whose profile photo was of her at her high school graduation, flanked by her deliriously proud parents, off-kilter mortarboard dwarfing her head.

That night I studied with Sara after dinner at the Starbucks located in the Garage, the mini-mall in Harvard Square that seemed to cater to high school potheads. You hadn't accepted my request yet. That was fine; maybe you were busy or took pleasure in leaving me in suspense. I tried to distract myself by reading even further ahead in the syllabus for my meeting with Samuelson.

"Why are you checking your phone every two minutes?" Sara asked. "What's so important?"

"I'm just nervous about this meeting tomorrow with Samuelson," I said.

She looked unimpressed.

"He's probably the most important English professor here, which basically means the most important one in the country," I added, and suggested we go home.

"You always sniff your jacket before you put it on," she observed as we packed up.

"Do I?"

"Yeah," she said. "Every single time. Does it smell or something?"

"Just routine, I suppose."

"I guess we're both creatures of routine," she said. "Or obsessive-compulsion."

I shuddered to think of the routinized trajectory we were on. If the two of us continued carrying on the habits that constituted our relationship, who's to say we wouldn't end up getting married, moving to Cleveland to be closer to her parents, and siring three children to replicate our family structures as I sentenced myself to a lifetime of buying CVS-brand zinc and date nights in mini-mall Starbucks.

While waiting to cross Mass Ave., cars whizzing past us, I had a sudden, unbidden image of pushing Sara into oncoming traffic.

You weren't home when we went to sleep, and you still hadn't responded on Facebook by the next morning when I knocked on Samuelson's office door in the Barker Center.

"Hello?" he said, apparently having forgotten who I was.

"David Federman," I reminded him. "Thank you for reading my essay on Ahab's primal wound."

That sparked some recognition in his eyes. He picked through a stack of papers on the desk.

"Yes, here it is," he said, adjusting his glasses and nodding. "That was wonderfully cogent. The peg leg as readerly misdirection in Ahab's pursuit of the white whale. A red herring, so to speak." Samuelson let out a scholarly chortle. He spoke in the same cadences in conversation as he did behind a lectern. "The analysis of the leg as a figure of castration is very nuanced; usually these things become somewhat over-the-top, especially from male critics. I'm teaching a seminar on Hawthorne next semester. Mostly graduate students, but I think it might interest you."

"That sounds up my alley," I said. "Or up my galley, so to speak." Samuelson chuckled again at the maritime pun. Wonderfully cogent, very nuanced. Six weeks in and already the star pupil in the Harvard English department. My fancy prose style wasn't going over Samuelson's head. It had finally found its proper audience, a potential mentor. I didn't have to be a lawyer; I could be a professor of literature, wear one of those jackets with patched elbows, stroke my beard in an armchair and apply nuanced close readings without breaking a sweat. You'd stand by my side at stultifying faculty parties and jet around the world with me as I was crowned with laurels at academic conferences, joking with the awestruck attendees and protégés about how impenetrably dense my books were while shooting me a private look that said you did, of course, understand them (I had taught you so much), these are the self-effacing comments we must make so as not to appear full of ourselves, when can we get out of here and fuck in our hotel room?

Samuelson's phone rang. "Excuse me, I have to take this," he said, picking it up.

"No problem," I said, taking out my own phone.

He cradled the receiver by his ear. "Thanks for dropping by."

"Oh, okay," I said, a little miffed all my reading prep was in vain, but that was fine—I would have plenty more opportunities in the spring. "I'll be sure to sign up for the Hawthorne seminar."

On my way out I stopped in the ground-floor Barker Café to order a cup of coffee. This is what a young literary mind did on campus: met with his professor in the morning and caffeinated himself for an afternoon of rigorous reading. I was about to leave when I noticed you in the corner, bowed over a table with your TF, Tom, presumably holding his own office-less office hours, with what had to be your—*my*—essay between you.

Riding high on Samuelson's praise, I approached, though it was a cavalier move. For all I knew, my Melville essay had made the grad-student rounds, and alerting Tom to our friendship could put us in academic jeopardy if he'd identified the writing in your James paper as suspiciously similar to my own.

"Hey," I said, standing over your table.

You looked up, uneasily, and casually pulled a notebook over the essay, as if to hide the evidence from Tom. Our little secret.

"Hi," you said.

"David," I said, addressing Tom. "I'm also in Prufrock. Harriet's section."

I paused to let him remember who I was.

"You're lucky, you got the best one." Tom scratched the underside of his beard. His eyes swerved to you. "The others tend to devolve into prurient discussions about nineteenth-century sexuality. Very juvenile stuff."

You giggled.

This wasn't how it was meant to go, with inside jokes from your section. You were supposed to ask what I was doing in Barker; I would blushingly admit that, well, I sort of just had my meeting with Professor Samuelson, I guess he wanted to see if I'd take his Hawthorne seminar in the spring; then Tom would say he was also taking it, he thought it was only for grad students, and he'd read my essay, too—well done, man, pull up a chair.

I waited for one of you to say something else.

"Your memory of poetry lines in class is impressive," I said to Tom. "It seems like you've read just about everything."

"I'm actually a robot," he said. "I have no soul."

Another giggle from you.

I evah on luos.

"Any chance you're taking Samuelson's Hawthorne seminar next semester?" I asked.

"No," he said, sipping his coffee.

There was another stretch of dead air.

"Well, I should get going," I said. "See you guys later."

"Nice meeting you, Dave," Tom said as I walked away.

After you had barely acknowledged me at the Barker Café, I wasn't going to make another appearance in your room until you accepted my Facebook friendship. I told Sara I'd been having insomnia and needed to sleep in my own bed for a few days.

By Tuesday my request remained unanswered. If your delay was calculated, it was no longer cute. I wrote an entire essay for you; all you had to do was click a button or press on a screen.

I waited outside Harvard Hall before Prufrock with my copy of

Sister Carrie. As you approached, I casually looked up and licked my finger to turn the page, my eyes briefly meeting yours before returning to the text, so captivated by my internal dialogue with Dreiser.

"You coming?" you asked at the door.

"Thanks," I said, stepping in behind you and up the stairs. Samuelson was making his introductory remarks as we entered the room and took adjacent seats in the back row.

I spent the first half of class reacquainting myself with your olfactory presence. Then, as you jotted down Samuelson's points about the amoral universe and deterministic plot twists of naturalism, you lifted a page in your notebook and readjusted your arm. Your left elbow, in the same black sweater as before, grazed the bottom of my triceps. My instinct was to reposition my arm out of politeness, but I resisted and stayed put. You left it there, the knob of your elbow applying faint, uneven pressure on me as you took notes with your right hand.

At first I thought you were unaware of it—and this was even more bewitching than the contact: that your indifference to others could translate into such corporeal obliviousness.

But you had to know. Maybe it was an accident initially, yet once it began, you were enjoying it, the subtle friction of two (clothed) body parts in public as a famous professor lectured. There was no one else in the room with whom you'd done this; I'd been watching, I would've known. You'd chosen me.

For the rest of class we stayed like this. Sometimes your arm would move to take notes farther down the page and create a centimeter of cooling space between us and I'd wonder if that was the end, but it wasn't long before your elbow reunited with my arm. In a way, this was the most satisfying ecstasy I could imagine, suspended in a limbo state of not knowing and partial touching, the morsel on the tongue though not yet down the gullet.

When Samuelson's lecture concluded, so did our dalliance: you abruptly withdrew your seductive joint and stood up to leave. The label of your sweater had flipped up and was poking out from the neck. ZIPPER & BUTTON, it said, upside-down and in reverse. NOTTUB & REPPIZ.

"Hey, did I add you on Facebook yet?" I asked as we bounced downstairs.

"I don't know."

"I feel like I did. Maybe a few days ago?"

"I always forget to respond to those."

"Here, let's put an end to your procrastinating ways," I said. "Go on now and respond to all your friend requests."

Outside, you turned to me, looking as if you were appraising me, wondering if you stood to lose any social status from accepting my invitation.

"All right," you acquiesced, taking out your phone. I peeked at the screen. You did, indeed, have a slew of pending requests.

"There," you said. "Now we're the best of friends!"

"Yeah, BFFs," I said with a laugh. "Or is it already plural, because it's 'best friends,' so just BFF?"

"Dunno."

"Well, have a good day," I said, pivoting toward Matthews, pleased with what my pushiness had accomplished. Ask and ye shall receive.

"You aren't going to walk with me?" you called out, sounding playfully hurt.

I stopped short. We'd already reached the endgame. I couldn't contain a giddy hiccup. All that ostensible apathy to the Facebook request, and you wanted me to escort you across the Yard, flame-colored leaves crunching underfoot in the brisk October air, as if I were a Harvard man of yore walking his Cliffie to class. You'd chosen me again.

"What?" you asked in response to my laugh.

"Nothing," I said. "I could kill some time."

We strolled toward Sever. "Want a cigarette?" you asked, rooting through your bag.

"Isn't smoking not allowed in the Yard?" I asked.

You laughed and lit up. "Such a rules follower."

"Sure," I said. "I'll have one."

You passed me a cigarette and the lighter. Trying to evade the inevitable coughing fit, I sipped a wine tasting's worth and spat it back out. It worked: a modicum of smoke I was able to store in my mouth that didn't infiltrate my lungs.

We crossed paths with a Crimson Key member regaling a college tour with the three lies of the John Harvard statue (that it wasn't modeled on its namesake; that the university wasn't founded in 1638 but 1636; and that John Harvard wasn't the founder but simply the first major benefactor). The centerpiece of the Yard, bronze symbol of educational aspirations, whose foot prospective students and tourists were invited to rub for good luck. (Harvard students, I found out upon arrival, sometimes urinated on it at night. *John Harvard peed himself!* I thought every time I passed it.)

I realized I was holding the cigarette like a joint. Fortunately, you were engrossed by the college tour.

"Ooh, sixteen thirty-*six*, not sixteen thirty-*eight*," you scoffed under your breath as the guide concluded his spiel with a camp counselor grin. "What self-aggrandizing bullshit."

I'd been one of those wide-eyed high schoolers, herded along with other antsy pre-frosh, crowding around the windowpane to catch a glimpse inside, sizing up the undergrads to crack the code, polishing John Harvard's urinous foot in the hopes it would lead to my acceptance. Maybe it *was* good luck: just a year later, and they were all watching me breeze past them, with you, as we mocked their naïveté.

"How'd you do on your essay?" I asked.

"I don't know. I haven't gotten it back yet."

"I thought you were discussing it with your TF when I saw you at Barker."

"I was," you said. "We were going over it. But he hadn't graded it yet."

"Did he have good things to say?"

"Yep."

"Cool," I said. "So, have you liked school this past week? And college? And how's your semester going?"

The small scar on your forehead rose quizzically. I felt a shock of glee whenever something I said catalyzed its ascent, proof of my existence in your mental universe. And it was such an elegant forehead: an otherwise unlined quadrangle, the hairline sharply delineated against the skin, bypassing the fuzzy no-man's-land that Sara had, whereupon it ceded to the sheltering forest of your locks.

"You pointed out people always ask how you like *Harvard*," I reminded you. "Never just school or college."

"Oh, that." You took a meditative drag and the scar returned to its resting position. "You know. My horizons are broadening. The foundations of my worldview are shaking."

I laughed too hard, a diaphragmatic bellow that sounded like an off-key horn.

And then a sobering sight: a hundred feet away, Sara walking to the library. That's right; her Chilean politics class had just let out. I was getting reckless—we'd probably missed her by minutes last week.

I bent down to tie my shoe, deftly plucking the laces loose first with my free hand, turned away from Sara's figure, and plugged the corner of my mouth with the cigarette. Leaning slightly so it didn't look like we were together, I took more time than necessary retying it.

When I stood up Sara was far enough away, with her back to us.

"There goes your girlfriend," you said, blowing smoke in her direction, wearing the impish smile from when you'd said *veritas*.

"Huh?"

You pointed with your chin. "Sara."

"Oh," I said, acting like I'd only just noticed her.

We pulled up to Sever. "Later," you said, grinding your cigarette underfoot.

"Later," I echoed, without the usual pang of loss when we parted ways. Now I could behold you from afar, on a screen, whenever I wanted.

In the privacy of my room I pored over your Facebook profile. There was no fodder for our budding relationship; you hadn't listed any favorite cultural interests or other groups, and the posts you'd written on your own wall were spare and logistical. So much for my plans of bonding with you over my deep knowledge of esoteric films or bands.

Instead I waded into the waters of your photogenic past, skimming over close-ups of food and panoramic sunsets to linger on images of you. The majority depicted your life before Harvard: European cities, what appeared to be your family's wrap-around-porched oceanfront vacation home, a couple from childhood (wobbly on skis; crying on Santa's lap), you and high school friends posing with tipsy hilarity at bars and nightclubs—entered with the benefit of fake IDs, I assumed, or city-girl know-how, or just because you were young and eye-catching and this was your Manhattan birthright.

The latest batch had been taken here, in dorm rooms and parties, with your handpicked beautiful people nothing like the factory-outlet Marauders. Several of the group shots featured you in intimate proximity to a guy I didn't recognize from your Annenberg crowd. He looked older than the rest of your cohort, the adult at the kids' table. His body language conveyed, more than mere ease, a sense of ownership: sturdy leg resting on coffee table, outstretched arms over sofa, squintily satisfied smirk.

Liam Barrows, he was tagged. His own Facebook page was private. All I could find on him was a single quote two years ago in the *Crimson*: "'The changes to the dining hall will have little effect on my eating habits,' said sophomore Liam C. Barrows, a resident of Adams."

So he was a senior; that's why he looked so much older than your friends. He could have anyone in the college, yet he'd zeroed in on a helpless-to-resist freshman girl, the sole demographic open to me. How greedy—like a billionaire winning the lottery.

When I came home from the library that night I heard music from Steven's room. "Always on My Mind" was playing on repeat. It was irritating, and I wondered if he had left it on accidentally. After the seventh cycle, I rapped on his door.

"One minute" came his voice from inside. The volume dropped and he appeared. His face was as pink as raw hamburger, his eyelashes matted and wet.

"You okay?" I asked.

"Ivana and I," he croaked, "we . . . we . . ."

He swallowed without finishing.

"You broke up?"

He closed his eyes and nodded as if confirming a death.

"Sorry to hear that," I said, and I was: his relationship with Ivana had kept him out of the suite.

The ends of his lips sagged gravely as he fought off tears. It was disconcerting to see him this way. I'd known Steven only to be relentlessly chipper about everything: the weather, whatever was on the menu, all the people he knew. ("Isn't he awesome?" he'd declare about each acquaintance who stopped by our table to say hello.)

He waved me into his room and crumpled into the bean bag chair, where he delivered a long-winded, unsolicited account of how his and Ivana's romance for the ages had met its demise.

It wasn't him, it was her. She didn't want to be tied down her freshman year and thought they should see other people. She felt like she couldn't breathe. She loved him but this was the best thing for both of them. Each cliché prompted vocal ruptures and a welling up. I responded on cue with my own platitudes lifted from movies and TV shows: he'd done nothing wrong, there were other girls out there who would appreciate him more, it was better to have loved and lost than never to have loved at all.

"She's the most beautiful girl I've ever known, inside *and* out," he said. "And she really *got* me."

Up to this point I'd managed to affect a look of sympathy, but here I nearly laughed. Forget the absurd notion of her contending with you for that title: Ivana was, by even the most charitable judgment, so distant from the winners' circle, way up in the cheap seats, that one might almost suspect Steven of mockery.

"She's cute," I said, "but the world is filled with cute girls. You'll find someone better."

"I don't want anyone *better*," he said. "I want *her*."

"I mean better for you."

He shook his head. "I don't want another relationship."

"Well," I said, "you'll feel better in the morning."

He nodded through his phlegm production. "I should call my mom back," he sniffled. "But thanks for being here for me."

"Sure," I told him.

As I headed toward the door, he stood and intercepted me with a hug. "You're a good roommate," he said.

"Not at all," I said, wriggling out of his embrace and ducking back into my room. "Oh, and if you wouldn't mind keeping the music down."

Steven recovered like an inflatable clown punching bag. "I realized we're not one hundred percent compatible, and I should find someone more suited to me, and so should she," he told me two days later. "And don't worry—we're going to make sure nothing's weird between us, so we can all hang out like before. Ivana and I decided the most important thing is the unity of the Matthews Marauders."

Thank God for small mercies.

On Friday evening Sara and I went to the Museum of Fine Arts in Boston. She kept asking what I thought about the European collection, assuming I was now an expert in the visual arts thanks to my Renaissance to Impressionism class. I answered to the best of my midsemester survey-course abilities but gave evasive or fabricated responses to questions that flummoxed me. To compensate, I pointed at a subway advertisement during our ride home.

"Look at that ad," I told Sara. "See how it shows just the woman's mouth eating the candy bar? It's isolating the one non-taboo main orifice, which takes in an edible object that becomes a phallic substitute. Now check out that bank ad. Male mouths are rarely eroticized. Instead, they're used to imply speech or some other kind of power."

"That's pretty insightful," she said. "Most guys don't pick up on stuff like that in everyday life."

I shrugged. "I guess I'm not like most guys."

"Yeah." She kissed my cheek. "You're definitely not."

When we reached Matthews my eyes traveled up to your fifth-floor window, warm with apricot light. You were home.

Our plan was to watch *Dumbo*; when Sara had found out I'd never seen it she insisted upon a screening. But first she had to finish editing a high school student's college essay. The tutoring organization she volunteered for matched Harvard students with Boston-area youth from underserved communities.

"I wish I could disable the thesaurus function from my kids' computers," she said. I looked up from my Dickinson book and at her screen, where she'd highlighted a sentence: "In college I will continue to prevail over my trials and tribulations and conquer adversity as I metamorphose my dreams into a reality."

"That's really bad," I said. "I hate to say it, but are you really doing a favor helping someone who writes like that go to a good college? Won't they be in over their head?"

"First of all, she's not trying to get into Harvard. Second of all, it's over their *heads*. And when you feel like criticizing someone, remember that all the people in the world haven't had the advantages you've had."

"I used 'they' because I didn't know the writer's gender. And I haven't had *all* the advantages. Compared to some people."

"You *have*, hugely," she said. "And I said 'all the people,' not 'all the advantages.' It's the beginning of *The Great Gatsby*. Don't you remember the opening line?"

"It's been a while since I read it. I think it was, like, seventh grade," I lied. "It's the last book on the Prufrock syllabus. I'll be re-reading it soon."

"You'll be *breeding* it soon?"

"I'll be *re-read-ing* it soon."

"You're a real mumbler, you know," she said.

We were lying on the bed, about to start the movie on her laptop, when you came out of your room. That was our riotous Friday nightlife on display for you: *Dumbo*, my Dickinson anthology on the floor, tickets for an upcoming performance of the Boston Philharmonic thumbtacked to the corkboard. Just a couple of unruly college kids.

"David," you said as you passed by. Sara and I looked up, both incredulous that you would address me. "Do you know what this week's reading is?"

"Emily Dickinson," I replied.

"Cool." You stepped into the hallway. "See you in class."

It was completely unnecessary for you to ask me, right then, as you were leaving to go out. You were throwing your weight around, letting Sara know she had some competition.

"I didn't know you were in class together," Sara said a minute into the opening credits.

"We didn't realize it until this week," I said. "It's a pretty big class."

I followed her to it during shopping period. If I could have, I would have signed up for her other classes, too. I stayed up all night writing an essay for her while I lied to you. I'm only here because she sleeps in the next room.

Feeling Sara's gaze on my face, I yawned.

"Did you guys sit next to each other or something?" she asked, yawning contagiously.

Yes, because I waited for her late arrival, and she intentionally rubbed her elbow against my arm, and she asked me to walk her across the Yard, and I saw you but tied my shoes so you wouldn't see me.

"No, we just saw each other when we walked out," I said. "Look, the movie's starting."

I snuggled closer to her and she dropped it. Sara teared up during the sequence when Dumbo's mother cradles him with her trunk through the bars of her cage.

"I should've warned you," she said, wiping her eyes. "I always cry during this scene."

The awakening of an erection. I was disturbed by the lack of obvious stimuli—the main on-screen visual was the animated elephants' non-pathetically phallic trunks—but when Sara's tears grew more pronounced, I noticed, so did my penis. To allay it, I looked at the nearby *Anti-Imperialist Marxism in Latin America*. (I'd gotten about a hundred pages into it by now, all during sessions on Sara's bed; it was more interesting than its dry title promised, an engaging primer on both specific Latin revolutions and the precepts of Marxism.)

"You didn't find that sad?" Sara asked when the movie ended.

"It's an animated kids' movie," I told her.

"You never seem to get moved by *any* of the movies or plays we watch."

"Who gets moved by plays?"

"*I* do."

"Guys don't cry during plays," I said.

She studied my eyes, as if plumbing their depths might solve the mystery of me. "You don't even *laugh* all that much. Like real laughs."

"I laugh at your jokes," I said, which wasn't entirely true. I always at least smiled at them, but it was a forced response to the concept and effort, and I often had to remind myself to emit a polite chuckle.

"I should hope so." She tapped my forehead with her finger. "Knock, knock."

"Who's there?" I asked.

"That's what I'd like to know," she said. "Who's *in* there?"

S'ohw ni ereht?

"No one," I said in the automatonlike voice. "I'm actually a robot. I have no soul."

"It's a joke," I added when she didn't react.

"I feel like there's a lot you bottle up inside," she said gently. "I wish you'd let it out with me."

"Would you really want some guy who's uncontrollably weeping all the time?" I asked, thinking of Steven after his breakup.

"Maybe you've got a point," she said with a short laugh. Then a hesitant undertone crept into her voice. "I told my parents about you."

"What'd you tell them?"

"How smart and thoughtful you are. How you're the one person here I feel like gets me."

"Thank you," I said.

"They want to meet you." She chewed her bottom lip. "I thought maybe you could visit Cleveland over winter break."

"Sure, that'd be fun," I said, imagining the bleak prospect of being snowbound in Cleveland with the Cohens. "Let's talk about it closer to the break. My family might be upset over losing time with me."

"Do *your* parents know about us?" she asked a minute later, shyly averting her eyes.

"Uh-huh." I hadn't spoken to my mother since that phone call before the Ice Cream Bash and had relayed only bare-bones, pre-dominantly academic data about my life over e-mail. "Well, just my mom. I figured she could tell my dad."

"And what did you tell them about me?"

"The same stuff, pretty much," I said. "Smart and thoughtful. Quotes Great American Novels to buttress her arguments."

She mussed the part in my hair. "Buttress," she said, smiling. "I should disable your thesaurus function, too."

She left for the bathroom with her toiletries. Reliably hygienic Sara, who always brushed and flossed and rolled on clinical-strength antiperspirant before bed. Sara Cohen, who wanted me to visit her and her family in Cleveland, the only one who wanted me to let everything out with her.

There was a lot you bottled up, too. I knew hardly anything about you beyond what I'd seen on the Internet. I didn't even know what your room looked like.

Without having thought it through, I found myself turning your doorknob.

I remained inside the doorframe. The swath of light that seeped in from Sara's room outlined a path to your bed, where creamy sheets lay rumpled under a white comforter. The walls were bare except for a single canvas painting with an abstract design. A Turkish rug sprawled across the floor, a few articles of clothing strewn about it.

Sara would be back soon. As I shut the door, something slipped to the floor on the other side. Your robe. It had slid off the peg attached to the door. After hanging it back up, I buried my nose in the interior folds, the material that had recently been in contact with your nude skin. Rubbing the belt, my fingers came across an imperfection. Upon closer examination, I discovered it had, at one end, its own small *VMW* monogram.

I extracted the belt from the robe's two loops, balled it up, and stuffed it in my pocket as a souvenir.

I was already between Sara's pink flannel sheets when she came back. As we carried out our nocturnal routine I thought of the silk resting in my pocket. When I ejaculated, I spasmed six times on her stomach, as if discharging a revolver of all its bullets. Sara reached for the shirt she'd demoted to a rag for the cleanup of these skirmishes. It featured an illustration of a feathered quill crossing a blade with the cursive inscription THE PEN IS MIGHTIER THAN THE SWORD. She regularly laundered it, but it built up a mushroomy odor between washings as it putrefied in its airless bedside-table drawer, and the blue cotton was now marbled with semen stains. *The penis mightier than the sword,* I thought with creative kerning each time it came out as I pictured the nib of a retractable ballpoint pen emerging like an uncircumcised penis.

The next morning I hid the belt in my drawer. But before I left for brunch I snipped an inch off the tip where the small *VMW* monogram was stitched, tucked it into the fifth pocket of my jeans, next to the Lactaid pills, and throughout the day I stroked it with my index finger.

I anticipated your reaction when I'd eventually "find" the belt under your bed. You wouldn't remember the missing monogram by then; you'd simply be grateful. How irksome it was to lose one small but integral piece from a larger item—a screw from an IKEA chair, the drawstring of a hooded sweatshirt, an ace from a deck of cards. Once it was gone, it could feel impossible to make the thing whole again, as if it were permanently doomed to a semi-functional life.

Chapter 9

Y ou shuffled in especially late to the next Prufrock lecture
and didn't sit near me. I caught your eye when class ended,
but you were the first out the door. En route to Sever you
ran into your black-haired friend Suzanne Marsh (Ilchester Place,
London; Marymount International School London). The daughter,
according to Google, of a famous British artist. The two of you pro-
cured cigarettes from your bags and stopped near University Hall to
brazenly smoke within spitting distance of the school's administrative offices. So you had time for her but not the guy who wrote your
paper.

As I approached, a student with a clipboard buttonholed me.

"Want to sign this petition to improve the benefits of dining service workers?" he asked.

"For the dining service workers? Sure," I said, loudly enough for
you to hear me, and scrawled my name.

"If you give your e-mail we'll send you updates on this and other
movements, too," he told me.

"Cool," I said, writing down a fake address before sidling up to you. "Can I get one of those?" I asked, pointing to your cigarette.

You took a long drag and handed me your pack and lighter. "Suzanne—David," you said, and exhaled through your nose.

"Ah, famous David," said gap-toothed Suzanne. It wasn't clear if this was sarcasm or if you'd actually discussed me with her.

"Nice to meet you." I clumsily pulled out a cigarette, lit it, and looked at you. "Did you get anything back recently?"

"What?"

"Did you get anything back? Like in terms of school?"

"It's okay," Suzanne said, directing a small smile at me. "I know about your little study session."

So you *had* talked about me with her.

"I got an A," you said nonchalantly, as if this were something you'd expected all along.

"An A," I repeated in a similarly measured tone, more pleased with this than I'd been with the A on my *Moby-Dick* essay. I puffed out an anemic em dash of smoke. "Congratulations."

"Thanks."

"David, are you free tonight?" Suzanne asked.

"He doesn't want to go to a final club," you said curtly.

"You're going to a finals club?" I asked.

"Fin*al* club," you quietly corrected me.

"Just a casual thing," Suzanne said. "Not a big do. Probably boring."

An invitation to an exclusive establishment with the elite members of my class—on a Tuesday night, no less, when all other Harvard students would be toiling away on problem sets and response papers. My foray into academic dishonesty was reaping unanticipated rewards.

⚜

"But I thought your Ethical Reasoning essay wasn't due till next week," said Sara, sitting cross-legged in sweatpants at her desk chair.

"It isn't." I thumbed through the Nietzsche reader I'd brought along with me for show. "But it's twelve pages and I want to get started now. I'm really sorry." I patted her on the head. We weren't much for physical affection, and I worried that anything more would come off as blatant overcompensation, the husband who gives his wife a bouquet of roses after consorting with his mistress.

"I'll give away my ticket and study with you," she said. "They weren't that expensive."

"Don't—you were really looking forward to the Philharmonic," I said. "Besides, I'll be distracted if you're with me, and I'm already anxious about it."

"But you *never* get anxious about work. It's actually kind of annoying."

She had me again.

"If I don't usually get anxious, it's because I plan ahead, like this." I summoned a wounded look. "I know you think everything comes easy to me, but I actually have to work hard. It's not always fun to be me."

She rested a hand on mine. "I understand," she said. "I'm the same as you, really."

"Why don't you invite that girl in your Chilean seminar you want to be better friends with?" I asked. "Lila?"

"*Lay*la."

"Layla," I repeated. "You'll have a much better time with fun new Layla than with boring old David."

"You're not boring," she said. "Or at least you're not old. Boring *young* David. Boring young David and Sara."

Grinning, she pulled the drawstring of her sweatpants taut and strummed it.

"I should get out of here," I said. "I'll see you at dinner, okay?"

"Okay, Grandpa," she said.

I arrived at the brick Colonial building near the upperclassman River Houses a few minutes before the time Suzanne had given me. I didn't know if I was supposed to ring the bell or wait for you, and couldn't see inside; the ground-floor windows were obstructed by curtains.

Standing by the entrance, I struck an indifferent pose as two girls came along and rang the bell. The door opened and they disappeared inside. A moment later it reopened and an Indian guy leaned out.

"Can I help you?" he asked.

It was well-known to everyone on campus, even the out-of-the-loop Matthews Marauders, that nonmember males couldn't enter a final club unless invited; women, on the other hand, just had to meet certain physical requirements.

"My name should be on the list," I said, sinking my voice an octave deeper. "David Federman."

"We don't have a list," he said. "Who are you with?"

"It's not a member," I said. "But—"

He shut the door.

Twenty minutes later it opened again, and this time you and Suzanne spilled out, unlit cigarettes dangling from your lips. Under the yolky haze of an overhead lantern your hair gathered warmer tones, the butterscotch yellows of my van Gogh wheat fields.

"Oh," Suzanne said, noticing me. "Did they not let you in?"

"I just got here." My new line for all denials. Not *I didn't do it* or *I don't recall* or *I can neither confirm nor deny* but *I just got here, I'm barely here, my restroom graffiti tag is "David wasn't here."*

Without my asking, you passed me the smoking apparatuses. This time I opened the flue of my lungs a little, not so much that I'd cough. I grew lightheaded and reverted to simulation. Even a fraudulently inhaled cigarette, I was discovering, conferred upon the smoker divided attention, an interior life more compelling than the one outside, alleviating the burden of generating conversation.

Suzanne hugged herself with her free arm and shivered. "It's fucking freezing out here," she said.

"Do you want my jacket?" I offered. I'd broken out my winter parka for the nippy evening.

Suzanne gave it a once-over. "Thanks, I'm all right."

"Okay, this is too cold," you said, flicking your cigarette into the street. Suzanne and I did the same.

A front of temperate air embraced us as we entered the building. It wasn't the human swamp that smothered dorm parties but well-stoked warmth, the cozy heat of hissing prewar radiators. "He's with us," Suzanne told the Indian guy.

This was no sophomoric party in a freshman dorm, with its frenzied frottage of ephebes like so many molecules in a chemical reaction, its deafening Top 40 songs, its disembodied arms holding out red Solo cups by the keg like baby sparrows squalling for worms. Upperclassmen mingled around button-tufted leather sofas and armchairs as the Kinks played at a soothing volume. Drinks were dispensed at a brass-rail bar. The walls featured framed black-and-white photos of notable alumni and vintage Harvard. From a far corner came the periodic crack of colliding billiard balls.

Having assumed there was a dress code, I'd worn the same outfit as I had to my college interview at New York's Harvard Club: a check-patterned button-down, my single necktie, beige chinos, and black patent leather dress shoes. But I was the only one in a tie. Hardly anyone even had a blazer. For the most part the guys were in jeans, sneakers, and boots. I contemplated loosening my tie, but worried this would call more attention to myself, an exhausted middle-manager father home from the office.

I trailed you and Suzanne to a secluded nook where, splayed over a sofa in decadent repose like models in a unisex fragrance ad, were three members of your inner circle: Christopher Banks, Andy Tweedy, and the angular blonde, Jen Pelletier.

"This is David," Suzanne said, omitting their names either out of laziness or inebriation.

They all looked up at me, then cut their eyes over to you and Suzanne as if to ask why you had invited me, why I had been granted entry, why I was standing next to you in public.

"Hi," I said. I received nods from Christopher and Andy and a raised glass from Jen.

Suzanne took a seat and you slipped off to the bar. I followed. A guy—presumably a younger member paying his dues—fielded someone else's complicated drink order.

"A shot of vodka and another vodka soda, when you get the chance," you said.

"Same for me," I added. He nodded over at us in confirmation.

"Thanks for inviting me," I said as we waited.

"Thank Suzanne."

"Either way."

You were facing the bar. From a distance, no one would know we were talking. You weren't the one inviting me; it was just payment for writing your essay. Maybe Suzanne had invited me only because she wanted me to write her own essays from now on, too. If I didn't engage you, the night would be a wash.

"So, vodka," I said. "My mom only drinks red wine. For the antioxidants."

You didn't respond.

"How about your parents?" I asked.

"What do my parents *drink*?"

"Yeah," I said before realizing how stupid a question it was. "No, I mean, what do they do?" You'd somehow dodged the question in the library, though I knew, of course.

"My dad's in finance," you said.

"And your mother?"

"A socialite," you said. "Quite the progressive arrangement."

This was more personal than anything you'd revealed before. Exposure begat familiarity begat intimacy. The next time we hung out here, you wouldn't care who saw us together.

"I hope you didn't have anything else going on tonight," you said. "I'd hate it if this disrupted any plans or anything."

"Nope, I was just doing work."

"Work, work, work. Got to be a good worker," you said. "God, I'm starving. Would you mind—" You shook your head. "Forget it."

"What?"

You turned to me and put on the squinching, apologetic expression of someone about to ask a big favor. "You know what would be so good right now? A slice from Noch's."

I estimated how much time walking to Pinocchio's, ordering pizza, and returning would take. "You want me to run over there and bring some back?"

"That'd be amazing," you said. "Could you also get me a decaf nonfat latte at Starbucks? Venti?"

"No problem."

"Do you need money?"

"No, I've got it," I said, not wanting to seem like a parsimonious Jew. "Any toppings?"

"Peppers, onions, and fresh basil," you said. "Oh, and black olives."

"Okay, so that's peppers, onions, basil, and olives, and a decaf nonfat latte. Venti."

You smiled.

"Did I not get that right?" I asked.

"I'm *kidding*." Your face lit up with manic amusement. It was so pretty that I didn't mind if the source was my gullibility. "I can't believe you were actually about to leave. I feel like you'd *murder* someone if I asked you to."

"Good one," I said.

"Like, if I asked you to murder Sara, would you do it?" You peered at me closely and spoke more quietly. "If we planned it in a way so you definitely wouldn't get caught? If I got someone who knew what they were doing to help you?"

You held your stare as I tried to formulate a response. The tension was broken as the bartender deposited our drinks before us and you laughed.

"I got this," I said, taking out my wallet.

"It's an open bar," said the bartender as you scooped yours up and took them back to your friends.

There wasn't enough room for me on the sofa, so I perched on the arm by your side. Christopher hovered over a book on the coffee table, a rolled-up dollar bill in his nostril as he vacuumed a line of white powder on the book.

A lifetime on the inside of a jail cell flashed before my eyes. (Ha.) I instinctively looked around the room for authority figures and the nearest exit. But it was dark and we were far enough from the action that others might not see it—should this even be considered illicit behavior within the debauched walls of a final club. And if I were going to get caught with narcotics, this would be the drug and the crowd with which to get busted. It might even be worth criminal charges to have this ace up my Never-Have-I-Ever sleeve.

I listened to the conversation—something about a party invitation that Jen never got—hoping for a way in, the tentative amateur trying to time the hummingbird rope cycles of double Dutch.

"Oh, it's in my spam folder," Jen said, looking at her phone.

"The spam folder is the collective id of late capitalism," Andy said.

Christopher sniffed with his head back. "Nice," he approved. He chopped a fresh set of cocaine vectors on the book with a credit card, pushed it over, and passed the dollar to you. Tracing the powder with the bill, you snorted it. I studied the procedure and began exhibiting the paranoid symptoms of cocaine use before having ingested any. You would all figure out I had never done it before, provided you even offered it to me. I didn't know which would be worse, a failed first attempt at recreational drugs in which I sneezed it out like a snow shower, or being denied them at such propinquity.

You turned to me and held up the bill. "David?"

"Yeah, sure," I said, like I'd just been offered a soda. You foisted the dollar on me. I rolled it between my fingers, this filthy, low-monetary-value portal into a high-value social sphere, and knelt in front of the table, hunched over the book (*Let Us Now Praise Famous Men*, by a Harvard alum, I knew, though I'd never read it). After inserting the bill—the same currency that a minute earlier had been inside one of your cavities—into my left nostril, the clearer passageway for my mildly deviated septum, I inhaled. It was easier than I thought, and I mimicked the others, tilting my head back when the line had vanished and continuing the insufflation.

I sat back down on the arm of the sofa and stared at my feet. I couldn't tell if the drug had an immediate physical impact on me, but regardless, it was a high. Just a few months ago I was watching TV at home during my senior prom. Now I was doing cocaine at a final club with the oligarchy of my class and sitting beside you. A regular Tuesday night for David Federman, Harvard edition.

Someone tapped my shoulder. I looked up from the floor and saw a groin not far from my face. Liam C. Barrows.

"Hey," he said. "Have we met?"

"I don't believe so," I said, the pitch of my voice rising with agree-ability as I stood. "I'm David."

"Liam." He shook my hand, which was consumed by his paw as he squeezed. The effect of his nearness to me was similar to yours, minus the erotic component; I felt he could X-ray my marrow, had an intuitive understanding of exactly how far below him I crouched.

But you appreciated intelligence and gentlemanliness. Liam was a brute, a government concentrator and taker of pass-fail gut courses if I ever saw one, a regressive banker in the making. You were smart enough to figure that out.

Christopher showed him the bag of cocaine. "Want a line?"

"No, I have to pace myself," Liam said. "Punch season starts Thursday and we've got events nearly every night."

So this was his final club, which would be hosting sophomores and juniors soon, recruiting the most desirable candidates and legacies for membership; I hadn't recognized its interior from any of your Facebook photos.

"Where'd you go?" you asked him.

"Can I talk to you for a minute?" he said instead of answering.

You made a face and stood, and the two of you disappeared around a corner.

"Trouble in 'Paradise Lost,'" Christopher said.

"Trouble in *gangster's* paradise lost," said Andy.

"Ben Stafford," Suzanne remarked with authority. "Liam thinks they were flirting before. But it was all Ben. She was just humoring him."

"Maybe so," said Christopher. "But she's certainly got the hot girl's need for constant male attention."

"You're such a misogynist," Suzanne said jovially.

Er'uoy hcus a tsinygosim. Words had been reversing in my mind with greater frequency and celerity lately. I was nearly getting back to my preadolescent facility.

Andy cocked his head in consideration. "Actually, I'd say Christopher's pretty gender blind in his contempt for people."

"And anyway, I don't think it's a misogynistic observation," Christopher defended himself. "It's the fallout of sending your daughter to an all-girls' school."

"You should've seen her at Chapin," Jen piped up. "She'd flirt with *any* guy that walked in the building. Totally indiscriminate. Even our Guido track coach."

(This was how your friends spoke about you behind your back, by the way. Now you know.)

I decided it was best to keep quiet and maintain a low profile so as not to betray my inexperience with drugs, final clubs, and socializing with anyone outside of the Marauders. I managed to elude scrutiny until Andy asked, without a transition, "Remind me, how do you know Veronica?"

Everyone's eyes found me. Now I felt coke-addled: heart palpitations, dry mouth, jittery leg.

"From class," Suzanne answered for me.

"Your guys' feminism class? What's it called, again? Women Be Shopping?" Andy waited for a laugh. "*Nutty Professor*, you philistines."

"Gender and the Consumerist Impulse," Suzanne said.

I hadn't realized Suzanne was also in the class. "English," I told him. I was going to leave it there, but wanted to prove I had a personality, that I wasn't just a body taking up space on the arm of the sofa—that someone was in here. "I'm pretty sure to take a feminism class here you have to be either a woman or flaming."

"Flaming?" Andy repeated in a campy voice.

"Excuse me," I said, smirking along. "*Queer.* I need to brush up on my microaggressions dictionary."

The joke didn't land. Andy and Christopher shared a glance.

"Can you believe we're already halfway through the semester?" Suzanne asked. They began gossiping about someone named Eliot as I grew insecure about my failed attempt at humor.

You reappeared without Liam. "I'm leaving," you announced, and grabbed your jacket. No one attempted to stop you as you stormed out.

"If they're done, I call first dibs on Liam," Andy said.

"That man is a beautiful specimen," said Christopher.

"No—a beautiful *species*," Andy said. "He's like his own category."

Only then did I realize why my joke had flopped. I wondered how best to redeem myself, but your departure was more pressing. Without a word I stood up and left.

You were marching down Mt. Auburn Street, cigarette in one

hand and phone in the other. Maybe it was best to leave you alone, judging by your brusque exit and speedy gait.

"Hey!" I called when you missed the turnoff to our dorm.

Spinning around, you looked taken aback, though I'm sure you would've been upset to see anyone at that point.

"Matthews is this way!" I pointed to the Yard.

"Shitty sense of direction," you muttered, walking back toward me.

Even with your drunkenness I struggled to match your steps for the remainder of the walk to our dorm, and my conversational gambits were met with grunts or silence. The night that had held the most excitement for me, ever, had meant absolutely nothing to you, and why should it have? You'd had hundreds of these evenings in the past, you'd have thousands more in the future, and you had no interest in a romantic present with me; you had Liam, a beautiful specimen and species unto himself. That you'd allowed Suzanne to invite me to the club without much of a fight probably wasn't indifference, I conjectured with cocaine-fueled reasoning. It was fear: you were afraid that I'd rat you out for plagiarism, though doing so would be incriminating myself. But mine was the lesser transgression, and therefore you'd offered me narcotics to even the score. Now you had something on me, too; if you went down, so would I.

As we headed upstairs in Matthews, your phone chimed, and in the scramble to fish it out of your bag, you stumbled and fell forward.

"*Fuck,*" you said.

"You okay?" I asked, bounding up behind you.

Trying to stand, you clutched your knee and moaned. You accepted my arm and gingerly rose to your feet, wincing with pain. I led you up the rest of the way, safeguarding you from another fall. First it was the accidentally-on-purpose elbow contact in lecture; already we had graduated to this.

When we reached the fifth floor, you listed in my direction and leaned slightly against me, your shoulders grazing mine.

"Are you okay?" I repeated. "Do you need to go to the emergency room?"

You shook your head no and whimpered. I became aroused.

"What is it, then?" I asked, my lips skimming your hair. You choked back a sob and I grew more erect.

"You wouldn't understand," you said, shaking free from my grip and limping down the hall to your room.

You'd allowed yourself to be vulnerable, for a few seconds, against my body. You weren't totally indiscriminate—not anymore, at least; you'd picked me for the role out of all available suitors. And even if you were, I would find a way to show you that I was much more than some guy who walked in the building—that you could tell me things, and I would understand.

In my room, under the covers, I revived my erection and cocooned it inside your bathrobe belt with an opening at the top. But I didn't want to bring myself to orgasm with it, as I usually did; no, this time I would use a light touch, just enough to sustain the engorging bloodstream, delighting in the tactile sensation and the memory of you on the stairs, extending my priapic ecstasy for hours.

But after a few minutes I was overtaken with eagerness and consummated my lust with the banal satisfaction that comes after getting what you so fervently want too easily.

Chapter 10

I was awoken the next morning by Steven passing through my room on the way back from the shower. Dripping wet with a *Doctor Who* towel around his waist, he stooped to pick something up.

"This Sara's?" he asked.

Your bathrobe belt. I'd carelessly left it beside me in bed as I fell asleep. It had slipped onto the floor overnight and was now dangling from Steven's hands.

"No," I said through a phlegm-clearing cough. As I reached out to take the belt, he retreated a step and examined it more closely.

"What is it?"

"I don't know," I said. "I just found it."

"Where?"

If I named a Harvard building, upstanding-citizen Steven would recommend I bring it to a lost and found. "Au Bon Pain."

"Mind if I take it?" He balled it up in his palm. "I'm learning this trick for my magic show in the common room Sunday night. I want to pull a long strip of material out of my mouth, and I haven't found anything that can fit inside."

He brought it up to his open maw.

"Don't!" I said. "Your braces will tear it!"

"What do *you* need it for?"

"A sweatband," I told him.

"You don't even exercise," he grumbled, dropping it on the floor as he proceeded to his room. I got out of bed and returned the belt to its proper place in the dresser.

That night at dinner, as I ferried my tray out of the food area, I considered ditching the Matthews Marauders and sitting down at your table with manufactured self-assurance. But that would raise understandable questions from Sara. Furthermore, the previous evening had been a bust with the others; I needed to focus on only you before trying to ingratiate myself with your group again.

And you seemed disenchanted with them anyway. As my tablemates debated whether they'd rather time travel to Renaissance Italy or Ancient Rome, you aimlessly twirled your fork in your pasta while resting your face on your fist, the graceful sweep of your jawbone meeting the sine wave of your knuckles. The distracted pose of someone wishing she were elsewhere, the same look you'd had that very first night at Annenberg, when I knew you wanted someone to rescue you, even if you weren't yet aware of it. Now you had a better idea.

"Speaking of Pompeii, anyone else worry that this place is a fire hazard?" Steven canvassed the table, where silently amused grins anticipated his answer to his own rhetorical question. "Its legal seating capacity is six hundred and seventeen students, and there are approximately sixteen hundred freshmen, not including staff. Granted, dinner stretches two hours and forty-five minutes, so the population density ebbs and flows, but there's still a high probability of exceeding carrying capacity at any given point—assuming, of course, that everyone's body mass averages out to predicted levels."

"Steven Zenger, everyone," said Kevin. "Steven Zenger."

The pronouncement of the full name; Steven Zenger was *such a character*, the type of guy who often said things *just like this*, that's *so Steven Zenger*, they'd grown to love him for his habitual expressions and quirks. None of my so-called friends, including Sara, had ever even said my surname. When they spoke my first name, they floated it charily, as if still unsure of it. What would precede a "David Federman, everyone, David Federman"? My lurking mutely in the hinterland of a conversation?

"What?" Steven smiled goofily, relishing the attention. "You don't think we all together have average-massed bodies?"

"Your mom has an averaged-massed body," Kevin said to more laughter.

"That's not even an insult," Steven said. "It's a compliment. You're saying my mom has a normal body weight."

"Oh, yeah, I forgot to tell you guys this idea I had," said Justin. "All my mom's e-mails were going into my spam folder, and I was going to fix it, and then I was, like, this should be an app."

Hilarity ensued.

"Mom-Spam," Kevin said in a smooth commercial announcer's voice. "For when you don't want to deal with your mom."

The hooting escalated.

"The spam folder is the collective id of late capitalism," I said.

Silence.

"*Okay*," Ivana said. "Now *that's* random."

After dinner I went back to my room, having told Sara I had to work more on my essay. I needed to let the air clear for a day or two. Raising the possibility of exposure so soon after the final club outing could shatter both relationships: Sara would want nothing to do with me, and you might independently decide you were better off without the complications I was adding to your dorm life.

But alone in my room I grew restless. You weren't allowed to be the one who called all the shots. I shouldn't have to be afraid of seeing you.

I knocked on Sara's door. "I realize I can just work here," I said. "And I'll sleep over, too."

You weren't home, it appeared. We spent two hours intermittently speaking, Sara at her desk, me on her bed reading for my art history class about staffage, the secondary, ornamental figures in a landscape.

"Oh, my God." She turned from her laptop. "Tiffany Gersh just friended me on Facebook!"

"Who's Tiffany Gersh?"

"We were best friends in elementary school, and then she grew breasts in seventh grade and became popular and dumped me. I hold her responsible for my low self-esteem."

"Huh," I said. "Kids are cruel."

"Especially middle school girls. And she didn't *just* dump me. She got all these other girls to pretend to befriend me one by one, then drop me and tell me I was a loser who'd never have a boyfriend or any friends."

"Sucks." I flipped the page of my book.

"You know who reminds me of her, a little?" She jerked her thumb toward your uninhabited room.

"Hmm."

"Did you ever have someone like that?"

"Fortunately not," I said. "Are you going to accept her friend request?"

"Yeah, right." Sara clicked her touch pad angrily. "I'm an extremely forgiving person, but screw her. She had all of high school to make amends."

A key jiggled in the lock outside, setting off contortions in my stomach. You entered without saying anything and vanished into your room, no signs of a limp. I was needlessly concerned to think my presence might be a problem. Of course you'd keep last night under wraps.

I finished my art history reading and took out my laptop to begin working on the Ethical Reasoning paper. I hadn't gotten very far when the lights in the room cut off and the hum of electronics ceased.

"What happened?" asked Sara. I quickly backed up my paper on my keychain flash drive. She opened the door to the hallway, where other perplexed residents fumbled in the dark. No lights out the window, either; the entire Yard had suffered a blackout. Within minutes the Harvard police were outside, urging us via bullhorns to stay indoors while they resolved the problem.

Sara had a candle in a jar and a matchbook on her bookcase. After lighting the candle, I held the match, letting it burn down just before the flame licked my skin. Then I struck another match and did the same.

"Don't waste them," Sara said when I went for a third match. "We may need more."

Your door opened and you poked your head out. "Hey, my phone died," you said. "Can you check if this is just Harvard or all of Cambridge?"

The Internet indicated that the blackout had hit a substantial portion of Cambridge. Hearing this, you stepped out with a bottle of vodka and another of club soda.

"Well, then, who wants a drink?"

I was shocked by the invitation, though I suppose no one wants to be alone during a blackout, and you didn't hang out with anyone else in Matthews.

"I should probably keep working while my laptop has a charge," said Sara.

"Oh, c'mon," you said. "It's a blackout. You're supposed to get drunk. David? You'll have a drink with me, won't you?"

"I could go for some vodka."

Sara's face turned to me with surprise in the flickering candlelight. "What the heck," she said. "One drink."

Even with Sara's presence, this was a chance to socialize outside of the library and a final club, with none of your friends or Liam around. Unexpected events could happen during a blackout, particularly if you mixed in alcohol. Dynamics could radically change.

You dipped into your room and returned with three Annenberg glasses. Sitting between us, cross-legged on the floor, you bartended. "That's good," Sara said, making a stop signal as you sloshed vodka into her glass. You passed us our drinks as we remained at our stations.

"Another wild night in Matthews," you said, holding up your glass in tribute.

"Yep," I said.

Sara's phone rang.

"Hi, Dad," she answered. "How'd you know? You have an *alert* set up for Cambridge? You're aware I'm eighteen years old, right, and I can handle a blackout? Oh, hi, Mom, didn't know you were there. Am I on speaker? Yeah, it's fine, safe in my room and my phone's fully charged. David's here, too. And Veronica." A pause. "Uh-huh, my roommate," she said more quietly, turning away from you. "*Yes*, I'll stay indoors. Call you tomorrow. Love you, too."

She made a quick kissing sound, as she always did when getting off the phone with a family member. "Sorry about that," she said with a sigh. "My parents are a little overprotective."

"That's sweet," you said. "You're lucky."

"Lucky?" she asked.

"You've got a nice family."

"You don't see us when we fight."

"Every family fights. But I bet your parents have a good marriage."

"They do," Sara said shyly. "They still hold hands and have all these little private jokes with each other. I suppose you're right. I'm lucky to have had that growing up."

"Not just growing up." You looked pensive, almost philosophical. "Also moving forward. It means you'll seek out healthy relationships."

Now *this* was encouraging. You were—internally, at least— pathologizing your relationship with Liam, just as I'd hoped. You didn't want to replicate the dysfunction of your parents' "progressive" marriage.

"It's natural for people to be attracted to the familiar," Sara said. "But it doesn't mean they're doomed to repeat their parents' mistakes. I'm not a psychologist, but I'd say recognizing that tendency in yourself is a sign you won't. It means you're aware of a potentially self-destructive situation and you'll avoid it."

You stared into your drink. "What if some people just have naturally self-destructive personalities?"

This question looked beyond the reach of Sara, whose closest brush with self-destructive behavior had been getting dessert when she was already full.

"Self-destructiveness is usually the product of low self-esteem," I said. "It comes when people think they don't deserve anything better from life, or that improvement is too hard. The important thing is to recognize that and make a change before it's too late. The real travesty isn't what's already happened, but resigning ourselves to it." I looked at Sara to salute her as my source for the last line.

"So for some people it's too late?" you asked.

"Well," I said, "I think there's a limited window people have to really change. After it closes, you're pretty much set with what you've got, unless you're the kind of special person who can rise above your circumstances. Most neuroscientific literature I've been reading in my Ethical Reasoning class backs this up."

"What the hell are you talking about?" said Sara. "Don't listen to David. He's a total cynic. *Everyone* has the potential to change. Not just *special* people."

How quick she was to stab me in the back and come to the assistance of the roommate who had spurned her all semester. Unprompted, you got on your knees and tipped the vodka bottle into her glass. I waited for her to protest, but she didn't. If anything, she looked flattered that you were now, whether out of self-pity or the uniting effects of the blackout, warming up to her. My veiled comment about how you should deal with Liam had backfired, inspiring the women to band against the tyrannical male in their sights. Should the two of you become friends, flouting history, it would be only a matter of time until Sara discovered what I'd been up to.

"Hey," you said, "we should get a photo of tonight."

Sara eagerly brought out her phone but frowned. "I don't have any space left for photos," she said. "Too many podcasts I haven't listened to yet. David, can we use yours?"

I consented. You stood next to Sara with the candle.

"You get in it, too," you instructed. "Sara's in the middle."

There was something disconcerting about your eager choreography. But I held the camera outstretched and snapped three photos with flash as you put your arm around Sara's shoulder, a smile stretching across her face. I could sense she was reconsidering Tiffany Gersh's request.

"Let's see," you said, and you both looked at the last picture. Our faces glowed ghoulishly from the flash and candlelight. After reviewing it you swiped the screen, sending it back to the previous one, and then the one before.

I remembered, with terror, what was in my gallery before this set: the picture of you outside Sever, smoking with Suzanne. In your burgeoning drunkenness, you might have mistakenly thought there was another picture of us all. The skyscraper I'd so carefully constructed would topple with one superfluous flick of your index finger.

"That's all," I said, exiting out of the gallery and bringing the phone to my hip. "I'm turning it off now to husband the power."

"Okay, you 'husband the power,'" you said in a fuddy-duddy voice. "I wouldn't want to frivolously 'wife' it all away." You turned to Sara. "So, how was the Philharmonic? It was last night, right? I saw your tickets on the corkboard."

"Yes, it was last night," she said. "It was really beautiful."

"Did you like it, David?" you asked.

"Yes," I said in a hurry. "I mean, no. I didn't see it. I was going to go, but then I had to work on this paper."

"Oh, that's too bad," you said. "So Sara had to go all alone?"

"I went with a friend," said Sara. "I understood. David's really disciplined about his work."

"What was the paper on?"

Your face was inexpressive in the weak candlelight but your tone was puckish.

"Nietzsche and ressentiment."

"What's it about?"

"How people from historically oppressed populations adopt a slave morality that pins the blame for their present predicament on their oppressor," I said.

"And what was your take, exactly?"

"I argue that even if their criticism is valid, their perceived victimization prevents them from looking inward and taking responsibility for their station in life."

"Sounds inspiring. Where'd you work on it?"

"Lamont."

"I was also in Lamont last night," you said. "Where were you?"

Sara looked puzzled by your sudden interest in my essay and whereabouts.

"The second floor."

"That's funny. Me, too."

I poured some vodka into my glass. "It's a big floor," I said, grateful for the cover of darkness.

"How long did you stay?"

"Practically all night."

"All night?" You jutted out your lower lip. "That's no fun."

"He's a workhorse," Sara iterated.

"Yeah, but college is about more than studying," you said. "You don't want to spend all your time in libraries like a perfect little Harvard student."

"He gets out," Sara came to my defense. "We do things."

"I'm sure he gets out," you said theatrically.

You were projecting your scorn for men onto me, making me squirm, trying to get me to confess or confuse my details. My white lie about where I'd been last night had triggered you, bringing up all the unresolved grievances you had with your father and Liam.

Mercifully, the interrogation ended there. "Well, guys, it's been fun," you said as you downed the dregs of your vodka soda. "But I've got to get out myself." You disappeared into your room and came back wearing your jacket.

"You're going out*side*?" Sara asked. "In the blackout?"

You put a finger over your lips. "Don't tell your dad."

"But you know you can't get into any dorms unless someone opens the door from inside, right?" said Sara. "And if your phone's dead, there's no way to call them."

"I'll figure it out," you said. "Actually, David, can you post one of the pictures of us to Facebook? I want to let people know I'm okay."

I turned my phone back on and drew up the last photo. "Wait," you said before I posted it. "Can I type the caption?"

I warily handed the phone to you, keeping an eye on its screen as you typed, "Hey it's **Veronica Wells** writing. Phone dead. Safe during blackout with roomie **Sara Cohen** and her bf **David Federman**."

You had publicly acknowledged me and the fact that we had hung out together. I would have altered the privacy settings to allow it onto my wall, except that any gains from my being with you were negated by Sara's position in the middle, with my arm around my "gf."

"G'night," you said, disappearing into the darkness of the hall.

"What was *that* about?" I asked after the door clicked shut, hoping to inoculate myself against the same question from Sara. "Why did she keep asking where I was working last night?"

"She was trying to make me question your credibility," Sara said.

I cracked my knuckles. "I was at the library all night," I told her.

"I know. Where else would you be?" As Sara giggled at the absurdity of an alternative scenario—the implausibility of disciplined, workhorse David doing anything other than studying alone in a library—part of me wanted to enlighten her as to exactly where I'd been and what I'd done.

"I get the impression she had a difficult childhood," she reflected. "Maybe it's hard for her to be around a happy couple, so she responds by trying to sow dissension between us."

"That's a smart insight," I said, and returned to working on my essay.

"Do you think she's pretty?" she asked.

"Do I think she's pretty?"

"Yeah."

I lifted one cheek in deliberation. "She's not really my type, but I guess she is, conventionally speaking."

"What's your type?" Sara asked brightly, joining me on the bed.

"You know," I said, leaning toward her. "Brown hair, about five foot three."

We kissed and I put the laptop away. Soon we were under the sheets, going through our paces more athletically than we normally did, from the vodka or the minor frisson you had sparked or the aphrodisiacal qualities of the blackout and lambent room. The dynamic hadn't radically changed with *you*—for the better, that is—but all variables were primed for the breakthrough needed to lose my virginity. I tugged at Sara's underpants.

"Not yet," she said, escorting my fingers away. "When I'm ready I'll let you know."

Grabbing the lotion, I thought of Liam Barrows coming downstairs to let you into Adams House but faltering on a step in the dark and battering his beautiful specimen of a body. I did my business, irritated with Sara's prudishness and her inviolable cotton undergarments. Not long after I came, the power turned back on, returning the room to brightness. Sara blinked in the harsh light before fixing her adoring gaze on me, as though I were the only person who mattered. The opposite of staffage.

The next day, as I was entering Annenberg for lunch with Sara, I saw you clearing your tray. Last night's encounter had left me unsettled, especially coming on the heels of the previous evening, which had ended so nicely; my sense of well-being was entirely dependent upon our most recent interaction.

"Shit," I said. "I just remembered I'm supposed to meet my Ethical Reasoning TF to discuss my paper."

"When?" Sara asked.

"Now!" I adjusted to a look of playful concern. "I hate to leave you on your own. Can you handle the Marauders without me?"

"I'll do my best." She raised her eyebrows and smiled slightly. It wasn't in Sara's nature to put people down, but it was clear she wasn't as infatuated with them as they were with one another. Maybe she, too, would someday muster the escape velocity to liberate herself from their gravitational clutch.

"So we missed a golden opportunity last night," I said as I pulled abreast of you in the Yard.

You startled at the sound of my voice. "We missed a what?" you asked, stepping up your pace a little.

"A golden opportunity." I looked around; no one was near us. "To murder Sara."

Your expression was equal parts confusion and horror.

"You brought it up the other night," I continued. "I assumed that was your plan. To get her drunk during the blackout, then murder her. You and me, together."

I waited a moment.

"I'm kidding!" I said. "Now *you're* the gullible one."

"That's funny," you said.

I bit my lip to control my glee. I needed to start acting like this more often around you—bolder, insouciant.

Walking in our direction was Scott Tupper with a friend.

"What's up, Veronica?" he said with a chin-up nod.

"Hey, guys," you said.

I turned my head after he passed and saw that Scott was likewise looking over his shoulder. For a second I thought he was scrutinizing me, his competition, or perhaps he had finally recognized David from elementary school. But he was simply checking out your ass. My fury was mitigated by the oddly consoling thought that you'd never choose yappy little Scott over strong, silent Liam.

"Seriously, though, you doing okay?" I asked.

"Why wouldn't I be?"

"You seemed a little off last night."

You didn't respond.

"And the night before you sounded kind of upset," I added. "At the final club. And after."

We were almost at Matthews. Sara would be at lunch for a while. Maybe we could continue the conversation in your room.

"It wasn't a big deal." You pulled a pair of earbuds out of your bag, inserted them, and plugged the cord into your phone. "I just drank too much that night."

"I know what that's like," I said.

"I have a meeting," you said, veering away from our dorm.

There was no *Excuse me, I've got to run,* no *Nice talking to you,* no *See you later.* I was a plaything you picked up when you wanted to be worshipped and callously discarded when you grew bored.

Back in my room, I got your belt out of the dresser and climbed into bed with my laptop to look at porn. My usual videos weren't doing it for me, though. I perused the panel of thumbnails on the side, clicking on one labeled "SPH," which I discovered stood for "small penis humiliation." An Amazonian blonde addressed the camera, laughing at the viewer's tiny dick and how it could never satisfy her, it was like a baby's, she would make me watch a real man fuck her.

It worked. I got hard, mummified myself within the belt, and indulged in a commingling of sensuous pleasure and fiery anger that, upon completion, promptly curdled into clinical disgust and smoldering shame.

These are the kinds of things to which you reduced me.

"Halloween is just an excuse for girls to dress like sluts," Sara told me. "And, yes, I'm aware that by using that word I'm complicit in their objectification."

After finding out that her new friend, Layla, was going to an upperclassman party up in the Quad, however, she decided to lift her boycott. She drew a map of Virginia on a shirt and bought a cheap wolf mask. The Matthews Marauders were also attending; at Steven's behest—and because it required no work—I went as him and he as me.

"But our clothes aren't distinctive," I'd initially protested. "And they're not even that different. No one will figure out we're going as each other."

"That's exactly the point!" He cackled like a criminal mastermind. "It shows how similar we all are underneath everything. We're just collections of matter that are constantly being recycled."

Despite her contempt for the holiday, Sara, ever the diligent student, became invested in her costume, sketching out neighboring states and drawing them to scale on the Virginia map after dinner. I sat on her bed wearing Steven's jeans and T-shirt (LET'S GET PHYSICS-AL).

You came out of your room in regular clothes, above the juvenile imposture of Halloween; you didn't need a costume to attract attention. Sara and I were among the mob of spectators who lined the parade route, sheepishly masking ourselves and wishing we were the anointed ones waving from the float.

"How late do you want to stay at the party?" I asked Sara before you reached the hall, so you would know we had, for once, exciting social plans, a *party*, we were young and hedonistic, who knew where the night might take us?

"Not too late," she said, and sneezed four times.

We trekked to the Quad with the post-pregaming Marauders as they concatenated inside jokes. Those real bonding moments, most of which I'd missed, had taken on mythic proportions in their retelling: when Ivana had eaten four sleeves of Oreos, the night they all stayed up and watched every episode of *Star Wars*, the time Kevin had passed out from drinking and they drew penises on his face and took photos.

Out of habit I reached for the snipped piece of belt in my fifth pocket, panicked when it wasn't there, and remembered that I was wearing Steven's jeans. Because they were tight on me, I'd put the silk in the more spacious but securely snug back pocket.

"Where's Carla?" I asked Sara as we lagged behind the others.

"She's going to Halloqueen," she told me. "The BGLTQ party." Carla had come out as a lesbian a few weeks ago and was spending more time at events hosted by that student group.

"I almost wish I belonged to a marginalized community so I'd have a safe space for all occasions," I said.

"The whole world is your safe space," she snapped.

"Not true. I shopped a feminism class and didn't feel particularly welcome there."

"I'm assuming that's a joke?"

"Fine, bad example," I said. "But I expect I'm going to be uncomfortable at this party, for instance."

"That's not about your identity; that's your disposition," she said. "And join the club, by the way."

We found the other member of our club hiding in a corner of the party. Layla's glasses kept fogging up in the steamy room, and every few minutes she took them off to wipe the lenses on the apron of her Raggedy Ann costume, during which time she turned her head when spoken to with the twitchy movements of a finch on the lookout for predators. The two girls had the fluid if formal rapport of a job interview that was going smashingly: bilaterally curious, overlapping interests, a dash of good-natured humor.

A football player was dressed up as the subject of the big news story that week: a pregnant Miami trophy wife who, it was alleged, had arranged for the murder of her husband for the insurance payout. Sara and Layla discussed her pending court case.

"It's really messed up how men receive almost all of the death sentences," I said.

"Are you saying she should get the death penalty?" Sara asked.

"Well, I'm against it in principle," I said, "but I believe in equality. She shouldn't get off just because she's a woman."

"Some people think he abused her," Sara said. "It's possible you would've done the same thing if you were in her position."

"That's ridiculous," I said, wishing I'd never brought it up. But I felt the need to stand up for myself. "Even if I somehow had it in me to *kill* someone, I'd never be the type to do it just for money."

"That's just it," she said. "You think you have to be a *type*. Maybe we're *all* the type, in some small way, and that's why we're so fascinated by the scandalous details, like whether she was having an affair with the guy who killed her husband or if she had a history of mental illness."

"I can't believe you're defending her," I said. "Did you see her eyes in the mug shot? She looks completely insane."

"I'm not *defend*ing what she did. I'm saying we're not thinking about her as a human being. We call her 'completely insane' and turn her into a thing you can dress up as for Halloween." She pointed at a zombie-scientist walking past us. "Just another monster."

Sensing I had lost the debate—if not for rhetorical reasons, then relationship ones—I volunteered to retrieve us all drinks.

Scott Tupper was present, dressed as Fred Flintstone. He had become the nucleus of a pack of boys that was seldom atomized. Tonight his arm was curled around the exposed lower back of a sexy Wilma. I could understand other guys being drawn to him, but it was bewildering that Harvard girls didn't find him noxiously repellent.

The room was exceeding its carrying capacity, to use Steven's term. It occurred to me that if somebody were to call out "Fire!" short Scott might be one of the victims of a stampede.

I refilled our drinks at regular intervals. ("He's such a gentleman," Layla gushed.)

Kevin lurched our way. "David!" he screamed in my face, spraying me with spit and shaking me by the shoulders. "David! You're *here*! You're actually fucking *here*!"

"Yep, I'm here," I said, trying to placate him. "I walked over with you."

He teetered woozily. "You're a funny guy," he said, and left.

We were all deep in our cups. Even Sara was speaking loudly and clumsily, more animated than I'd ever seen. A few times she slurred her delivery—"the Scandanissas—wait, *nist*—the *Sandinistas!*"—and doubled over in hysterics.

When Layla went to the bathroom, Sara looped her arms around my neck and rested her head on my chest, rocking off rhythm to the up-tempo song. I pulled closer to her to avoid being hit by an unbridled dancer and, interpreting this as a romantic gesture, she craned her neck and puckered her lips. We'd never done this before in full public view. She kissed with the suction of an airplane toilet's flush.

"You taste good." She licked her lips in an unprecedented display of sexual initiative. "Like alcohol."

"Let's get out of here," I proposed. If there were a night to expand our bedtime repertoire, this was it. "I want to have you all to myself."

"All right, mister." She shimmied her shoulders. "Where'd Layla go?"

"To the bathroom," I reminded her.

"We have to wait for her," she said. Raging drunk and still unfailingly considerate.

We continued swaying and kissing. I closed my eyes as the music throbbed around us and the alcohol gave me the floating sensation of riding in a car over a bump, feeling lordly for once at a party. I was making out with a girl on a dance floor in college. Then I remembered that moment at the final club when I realized you were facing the bar to make it look like you weren't speaking with me. To avoid slipping down a rabbit hole of self-doubt, I recalled our parting that night, you crying in my arms. But then you were cold to me, if not outright hostile. Your mercurial nature was maddening, absolutely maddening. The next time the pendulum of your affections swung my way, I'd take hold at its apex and not let go.

Sara's arms came down and she burrowed her hands into my back pocket, squeezing my butt. When she withdrew them she was holding the snipped piece of belt.

"VMW," she read from it, one eye closed, and looked up at me for an explanation.

"*BMW*," I said, grabbing it back from her and wedging it in the small pocket so she couldn't take it out again. "You're not seeing straight. We should get you home."

"Yeah," she said. "Let's ride in your BMW all the way home."

Back in Matthews, Sara collapsed on her bed. After removing

her shoes and outerwear and turning on the white-noise machine, I undressed myself. I recollected Steven's gloating appeal to keep his family photo on my bookcase and entertained the notion of subbing out THE PEN IS MIGHTIER THAN THE SWORD for LET'S GET PHYSICS-AL.

But tonight no shirt would be necessary. Sara was drunk. So was I. We had both soaked up the collective id of late capitalistic Halloween. I'd waited long enough. I kissed her. She kissed me back and I pressed my erection against her. "Let's just be naked together," I said, hooking my fingers under the waistband of her underpants. This time she didn't object. I rolled them down her legs.

In the midst of a kiss, I allowed the tip of my penis to graze her crotch. She shivered and clasped her hands tighter around my back. I paused and did it again, this time drawing out the contact. After the third pass I whispered, "I want to be inside you."

"We should wait," she said, sounding more sober.

"But it feels so good," I said, poking at an oblique angle. "And I want to feel close to you in a way I haven't before." It came off as a cheesy line. I needed something heartfelt.

"I love you," I said. The words tumbled out with strange ease. I hadn't told my parents I loved them since I was a child.

The sounds of our breathing. The rumble of her white-noise machine. The clanking of the radiator.

"I love you, too," Sara said.

I evol uoy, oot.

I cautiously rejoined our bodies.

"I don't know if I'm ready," she said.

"We'll take it slow," I promised her, gripping my penis and manually rubbing it up and down her vagina. She was wet and didn't say anything as I guided myself inside.

I won't lewdly describe the sensation. Greater than the physical pleasure, anyway, was the gratification of clearing away the stigmatized reek of virginity I emanated.

"I want to come inside you," I whispered into her ear. She didn't protest, and so I did, in a gloriously undammed eruption whose aftermath felt so unlike the disgrace that typically accompanied my self-inflicted climaxes. This was more akin to extricating a slimy clot of hair from a sink drain and watching the filthy standing water swirl out of sight with a satisfying glug.

And with that, my chronic ache for you felt a little less acute. I was a copulative agent now, same as you, inducted into the society of those who practiced physical intimacy in its most classic form. You weren't towering above me anymore.

"Have you done that before?" I imagined you asking, our limbs tethered in a postcoital clutch.

"Of course," I'd say, and it would be true.

Chapter 11

In the morning Sara seemed aloof, or maybe bashful; she didn't mention anything about the threshold we'd crossed hours earlier, and I wasn't going to bring it up. Perhaps it was the result of her vicious hangover. Or maybe it was her attempt to mirror my cool, which she likely attributed to my veteran reaction to intercourse: the emotionless junction of anatomies, a mercantile transfer of bodily fluids, nothing worth making a fuss about.

Yet inwardly I was rejoicing over my new status, estimating how many of the other freshmen in the dining hall were virgins—those sad, perfect little Harvard students who spent all their time in libraries. Indeed, there was more to college than studying.

I went to Sara's room that night, hoping to repeat our performance and to see you. Neither event happened. Though we still didn't discuss having had sex, upon getting into bed she mentioned that she was having painful premenstrual cramps. I took the hint and we went to sleep.

Only three more weeks until our next paper was due in Prufrock.

Based on the successful results of our first collaboration, I expected another request for assistance. I just needed to go through the motions a little longer with Sara.

That Friday evening we saw *Macbeth* at the American Repertory Theater, with Layla as a third wheel, and went afterward to a nearby café for tea. As we waited in line, I observed a cat—I assume the owner's—staring with a stoner's intensity at a heating vent. Eventually a cockroach crawled out of the vent, and the cat lunged. But instead of killing it, it pawed the insect around, curtailing its path in every direction.

I nudged the girls and pointed. Layla looked disgusted; Sara, distressed.

"Don't watch," Sara said, turning away. "It's upsetting."

The cat flipped its quarry on its exoskeleton and, as the cockroaches' legs waved feebly in the air, enjoyed the spectacle for a few moments before further torturing it.

My attention was diverted by a familiar voice at the front of the line. Tom the TF. When he was done placing his order, I stepped forward to say hello. This was what I had imagined my life here would be like: bumping into people I knew wherever I went, even grad students.

"Tom," I said as Sara and Layla spectated. "It's David."

He looked as if he were trying to place me.

"From Prufrock," I added to jog his memory. "Not your section, though."

"Nice meeting you," he said.

"We actually met a few weeks ago. At another café, in fact—the Barker Café." I forced a chuckle. "You made the joke about how your section devolves into prurient discussions about nineteenth-century sexuality."

He thought for a couple of seconds. "Oh, right-right-right," he said, seemingly less self-possessed out of a classroom context. "This is my wife, Lucy." He put his arm around the woman by his side. "And I'm sorry—remind me of your name?"

"David." Though not in the same league as you, his wife was sleekly attractive, and it baffled me that she'd be with Tom. Ever since the Barker encounter, I'd found his comments in Prufrock—especially the sardonic ones—increasingly smarmy. He wasn't even that good-looking; he just carried himself as if he were.

"Are you an English grad student here, too?" I asked.

"No," she said. "I teach comp lit at Colby in Maine."

The barista set two lidded cups on the counter. "And she's been driving all day," Tom said, grabbing them. "So we should get going. Have a good weekend."

After our orders came we took a table. I had a hot chocolate with soy milk and Sara and Layla shared a pot of decaf green tea. Sara dispensed quarter cups at a time so that it wouldn't lose its heat, thwarting any burns by vacuum-sipping the liquid's surface. The girls talked about their elementary school drama careers, one-upping each other with tales of botched lines and missed stage cues.

"I wish I could act," Sara said wistfully. "Not for plays, but because it would have benefited me in a number of life situations. David, try my tea, it's really good."

She poured a fresh serving and passed me her cup. I took a gulp, singeing the roof of my mouth, and loudly sucked in cool air through my teeth.

"Is he okay?" asked Layla as I rocked in discomfort.

"He's fine," Sara assured her. It took some time for me to recover, and when I did, Sara gave me a tender pat on the head. "It's a good thing you'll never have to endure childbirth." She turned to Layla. "David doesn't have the highest pain threshold."

"What are you talking about?" I asked.

"You know," she said. "You're always whining about the littlest things."

"No I'm not."

"It's okay that you're sort of delicate," Sara said, now rubbing my back. "I'm not the kind of girl who needs her boyfriend to be some manly soldier."

"Did you ever act in high school, David?" Layla politely inquired, trying to head off a lovers' spat.

My last theatrical role was a nonspeaking part as an anonymous Pilgrim in a fourth-grade Thanksgiving production.

"Actually, I was in *Macbeth* senior year," I said.

"You *were*?" Sara said. "Why didn't you say anything?"

I shrugged.

"What part were you?" Layla asked.

"Macbeth."

"*David!*" Sara laughed. "You *played* Macbeth last year, and we just *saw Macbeth*, and you didn't mention it all night?"

"You didn't ask."

"You must be a really good actor if you got cast as Macbeth," Layla said. "What else were you in?"

"That was it. I only auditioned for it because my girlfriend was Lady Macbeth—she was the female lead in all the plays—and I always said I didn't think acting was that hard, so she dared me to audition." I was surprised by how easily the backstory came to me, reinforcing—*buttressing*—my previous lie to Sara about Heidi McMasters. "Then, when I got the part, I had to go through with it. The drama teacher kept hounding me to act in the spring production, but I didn't want to. I couldn't stand the theater kids. Acting's for people with no real personality of their own. Just ventriloquists for other people's ideas."

"Huh." Sara smiled, looking at my face as if hoping to glean all the other secret talents I had yet to divulge. "You think you know someone."

When we were home, Sara asked me to scratch an itch on her back. She lay facedown on the mattress and pulled up her shirt.

"You've got a blackhead," I said as I raked my fingernails over her skin. To my surprise, she asked me to pop it. These were the familiarities you broached, I supposed, once you'd had sex. I pinched the decimal point until the head crowned and a thin brown pill sprouted out. It would have repulsed me if I didn't take such pleasure in its extraction.

"Got it," I said.

"*Ooh*, show it to me," Sara squealed, turning her head around to take a gander. Bearing the fragile specimen on my index finger, I reached in her direction.

"Hold it under the light," she demanded, scooching toward her bedside lamp. I moved my hand beneath its heat and she squinted with shameless fascination at the dark, bulbous root. She looked disappointed when I flicked it with my thumb into the trash.

"Are there more?" she asked, pulling up her shirt again.

"No," I said without looking.

We got in bed and her whispery snores picked up within minutes of turning out the light. I lay there contemplating her willingness to have me extirpate her impurity, unable to fathom letting anyone—even Sara—examine at such close range my own vile subcutaneous matter.

I was on the crumbly precipice of sleep when you entered, briskly slipped into your room, and reemerged soon with your toiletries. Once you were gone I removed myself from the bed, careful not to rouse Sara, donned the mesh shorts I kept at her place for bathroom runs, and stepped into the hallway, shutting the door behind me. I stood there waiting for you to return. Finally the bathroom door opened and you appeared. Preoccupied by your phone, you inched your way down the hall.

"I got locked out," I said as you approached. "She isn't hearing me knock over her white-noise machine and I don't want to wake up the hall."

You briefly registered me and returned your attention to the screen.

"Very thoughtful of you," you muttered, typing away. "You two have such a wholesome thing going on. Together every night. Happily ever after."

"Something like that," I said.

"I wonder what that's like."

"A healthy relationship?"

You continued to thumb the screen aggressively. After a long break you spoke almost as though you were talking to yourself and had forgotten I was there. "Being attracted to nice guys and not self-centered assholes."

It took me a moment to come up with a reply.

"People are more complex than simple binaries," I said. "The assholes usually have a little niceness underneath. And the nice guys have a little asshole to them."

"Do they?" Your lips curled coquettishly. "The nice guys?"

"Some of them."

"And would you put yourself in that category? One of those assholish nice guys?"

The hall was silent except for the apiarian buzz of the overhead light. I canted my head, as if somewhat abashed by the classification. "Others have."

Your phone vibrated. You closed your eyes before looking at the screen, bracing yourself for bad news. But then your face brightened when you opened them and saw who it was.

"Hey, you," you answered quietly, turning to unlock the door. "I thought you couldn't talk." You walked in without holding the door for me. I caught it just before it swung shut.

Back in Sara's room, I thought about flinging your door open like an outlaw in a saloon, striking the phone and Liam's voice out of your hand so I could show you how feral my desire was, that I wasn't the wholesome nice guy you assumed me to be.

Then I reassessed what had just transpired. The way you'd spoken to me was still major progress, the culmination of two months of meticulous strategizing, a beautifully arced shot into the corner of the goal after a cat's cradle of short, precise passes and incremental gains in field position. I had gotten this far through patience and caution, taking calculated risks, not through brute strength.

I shed my shorts and eased into bed. Sara's body turned in sleep. I pictured you behind your door, telephonic captive to Liam, and slid my hand under old reliable RAISE OHIO'S MINIMUM WAGE NOW! to fondle her left breast. She shifted again. My hand sauntered down her stomach. She palmed my wrist and dazedly murmured something I couldn't hear.

"I want you," I said, uncoiling my index finger and prodding her on top of her underpants.

"David," Sara said, now awake. "Not tonight."

"But I want you so badly," I repeated, putting my weight on top of her.

"I'm at the end of my period."

"I don't care," I said, and mashed my mouth against hers. I rolled her underpants off. When I tried to penetrate her, Sara spoke up, but not to demur.

"My tampon's still in," she said. I looked away as she took care of it.

Up until now I'd been mute in all our bedroom activity except for the small glottal exclamation I'd allow myself at the conclusion. But tonight I wanted to be loud, to be heard by Sara, by all of Matthews Hall and Harvard Yard and Cambridge, and, most of all, by Veronica Morgan Wells.

"I love fucking you," I said, a notch above a whisper, a golf commentator narrating the putt. I found my hand moving to Sara's soft throat and massaging it.

"I love fucking you," I spoke at normal conversational level, our moans alternating with the cheap *squoink*ing institutional bedsprings, her eyelids shut and quivering.

Then I closed my own eyes and imagined you beneath me—in your white bed, your canvas painting leering at us lasciviously, the air sugared with your lavender fragrance—as my other hand drifted up to Sara's nape and my fingertips touched with room to spare around her slender neck. When I climaxed I cried out in my loudest voice yet, enough to call someone's attention from across a crowded room, only this time I reversed the second and third words of "I love fucking you." And I wasn't calling it across a crowded room. I was calling it through the wall.

You'd speculated about my romantic personality and you'd now heard me having intercourse. No more measuring out my life with coffee spoons; it was time for a paradigm shift. Breaking up with Sara the morning after sex would be too harsh. And you were still asleep anyway. The real coup would be if you overheard it. Not only would it alert you to our severance, one that I'd initiated, but if Sara became distraught, it might make David from Prufrock look a little danger-ous, not so wholesome after all.

That night, during dinner, I asked Sara when she wanted me to come over.

"Maybe we should take the night off," she said. "I'm feeling kind of out of it."

"No problem," I said.

On the walk home to Matthews I saw your light was on. I said good night to Sara at the fourth floor, waited a few minutes, and marched upstairs and knocked on her door.

"We're on a break tonight, remember?" she said.

"I know. But I need to talk to you about something."

She looked mildly chagrined but let me in and went to her desk chair. I sat on her bed, leaning against the wall that separated your rooms, and exhaled forcefully to communicate that what I was about to say was the culmination of much agonizing soul-searching.

"I don't think this relationship is working," I began.

She seemed more incredulous than upset. "You're breaking up with me?" she asked, almost laughing.

I looked down and slowly nodded to myself. "I don't think we're right for each other. We're different people. We want different things."

I paused as a siren wailed from Mass Ave. then faded.

"I've been grappling with this for a while," I continued. "I was hoping time would prove me wrong. But I guess I can't change the way I feel deep down."

"How exactly is it that you feel?"

"Like I can't breathe," I said.

She sat next to me on the bed. "And *this* is when you choose to tell me? You couldn't have done this, say, last night before we went to bed? Or, better yet, last week?"

"I realized it wasn't fair to keep you in something that I wasn't fully invested in."

"'*Invested in*,'" she repeated bitterly. "Is it because we had sex? Have you lost your *investment* now that you've had me?"

"Of course not," I said, which was technically true. "It's not anything you did; it's me. There are plenty of guys out there you'd be better off with, maybe guys you wouldn't consider because you were with me. I don't want to hold you back from that."

"Ugh, stop with the clichés!" she said. "Are you reading from a script or something? Now I'm wondering if you ever actually felt anything—if you even cared about me."

My eyes fell on *Anti-Imperialist Marxism in Latin America* on her bookshelf. I hadn't gotten to finish it and never learned the outcome of various proletariat revolutions.

"I'm doing this *because* I care about you," I said softly, recognizing that they weren't the words of a dangerous asshole so much as a generically noncommittal male.

"No," she said stoically. "You don't care about me. I don't think you're capable of caring about anyone besides yourself."

"I'm not sure where you're getting that."

"You're missing whatever it is that makes you feel things for other people," Sara said.

She was wrong. My feelings were stronger for you than for anything else in my life, though I couldn't refer to that in my defense.

"Sometimes I have no idea who you really are," she went on. "I feel like I projected all these qualities I wanted onto you."

Prohibited from using platitudes, I had nothing. She buried her face in her pillow. "Would you please leave," she said meekly. "I don't want to see you right now."

"Sara," I pleaded halfheartedly.

"'*Like I can't breathe*,'" she said, freeing her mouth from the pillow. "Really nice."

"Well, I'm sorry I'm not the nice boyfriend you thought I was!" I shouted so that you had to hear it.

I let myself out and waited on the other side of the door until I heard her sobs, instigating the familiar movement in my boxers. Back in my room, I lay on my bed as rollicking bands of revelers streamed below my window on their way to Saturday-night destinations, off to share scorpion bowls at the Hong Kong on Mass Ave., to clink shot glasses in the River Houses, to trade bon mots during punch season at the final clubs.

No matter. You had heard me reject Sara, and you had heard her cry. I was someone who had the power to wound another person.

Chapter 12

For the next several days I kept a low profile, skulking into the dining hall at odd hours and sitting alone at an outpost with my books. I managed to duck Sara in Matthews, too, and studied in out-of-sight carrels in Widener.

One night, tired of eating by myself, I knocked on Steven's door.

"I'm getting sick of Annenberg food," I said when he opened it. "You want to go to Noch's? It's on me."

"Um." He bent his spindly arms and massaged his knobby elbows. "I hate to be the bearer of bad news, but because Sara's the one who got dumped, we felt we should support her right now."

I hadn't considered this consequence of our breakup, assuming that, after a few days, Sara and I would broker a détente and the unity of the Matthews Marauders would be, as ever, preserved.

"But the two of us getting pizza doesn't involve Sara."

"Well, there's also . . ." He reached around himself and scratched his upper back. "I don't know how to say this exactly, but there was some stuff about you? Stuff that was said, I mean?"

"What sort of stuff?"

His face scrunched up in a rare expression of social discomfort. "That, with Sara, before you broke up . . ."

I'd never seen Steven hem and haw like this; he was incapable of embarrassment for himself, but it seemed that he was embarrassed for me. Had Sara said I wasn't good in bed? That I'd clearly lied about not being a virgin? I'd wanted to be the kind of person people gossiped about, but not like this, with who knew what grinding through the freshman rumor mill.

"What did she say?"

"That you crossed a line," Steven said.

"Crossed a line? What line?"

"Apparently"—he examined his fingernails—"she didn't really say yes."

Though he swallowed the final word, it sounded louder than the rest. I thought back to our latest encounters and replayed their limited dialogue.

"She didn't explicitly say no, either," I told him. "And, not to get too graphic, but she took out her tampon."

Steven put up his hands. "I don't want to get in the middle of anything."

"She took out her tampon!" I repeated. "Explain to me how that's not saying yes!"

He didn't respond.

It wasn't like Sara to confide such personal details to the Marauders. "She told all of you this?" I asked.

"Just Carla," he said. "Then Carla told the rest of us."

I imagined Carla sharing the misinformation at the next BGLTQ meeting, all her "allies" shaking their heads at my purported wrongdoing, but isn't this what we've come to expect?

"I could meet you at Noch's after dinner," Steven offered. "I'll have eaten already, but I can sit there with you for a little bit." The pitiableness his charity ascribed to me made me feel worse than if he'd said he never wanted to talk to me again.

"That's okay, I'll be fine," I said abruptly, and told him I had to study during dinner anyway. I did just that, choosing Annenberg over Noch's to prove I didn't have to cower from calumny, taking visual sips across the room of Sara to gauge if she was further slandering me. Once in a while she nodded solemnly, as if confirming that, yes, I had done terrible things to her, even more horrific than she'd previously let on.

But I was being paranoid. No real line had been crossed. This was college. People had sex. They didn't just hold hands and masturbate.

You cut the next Prufrock. The following week featured Tom's guest lecture on *The Sound and the Fury*, an intellectually posturing performance full of verbal pyrotechnics, signifying nothing. You sat in the front row with the rest of your section, laughing along at his pandering pop-culture references.

When it was over I waited for you outside Harvard Hall. "How's it going?" I asked, falling in step with you over to Sever.

"All right."

"Sara and I broke up," I said. "That's why I haven't been in the room for a while."

"That's too bad," you said in your usual affectless tone.

"Yeah. She took it pretty hard." I inhaled deeply through my nostrils, as if I were reeling with guilt over the pain I had inflicted on your devastated roommate. "Anyway, do you want to meet up sometime to work on next week's essay?"

Before you could answer, someone called your name across the Yard. Liam took his time walking over to us. I scuttled away a few feet as he parked his hands on your hips, pulling you against his midsection. Your head came up to his chest. After whispering in your ear he smiled and leaned down to kiss you. Your lips closed instinctively as he forced his against them. It reminded me of when

Sara tongued me, the instinctive desire to shield an orifice from a probing foreign object.

"I gotta run," he said, lacing his fingers in yours as he took a reluctant step back. "But I'll see you at the thing tonight. Come any-time after nine."

"I don't think I can make it tonight," you told him. "I'm sorry—I'm totally behind in my work."

You appeared less contrite than apprehensive. He nodded slightly and pursed his lips as if he'd anticipated this excuse.

"Babe, I can't help it if everyone's assigning essays before Thanks-giving," you said.

"Why don't I stay in with you, then. I've got some reading."

"Okay." Your voice was a little unsure. You turned your head and looked over at me. "David'll be there, too," you said cheerfully. "He's helping me with my paper. You remember David, right? He came to the club a few weeks ago?"

Liam looked my way. I lifted my forearm, my parka's sleeve mak-ing a waxy sound, and flashed a palm in his direction.

"What class is this for?" he asked, alternating his gaze between the two of us.

"From Ahab to Prufrock," I spoke up. "Tragically Flawed Hero(in)es in American Literature, 1850–1929."

"My English class," you translated.

"Fine," he said. "I'll leave you two to your study date."

"Tomorrow night I'll come over, I promise," you said, stroking the back of his neck and rising to your tiptoes for a parting kiss.

My breakup with Sara had paid off. Maybe she'd even told you about the line I'd "crossed," thinking it would cast me in a negative light—except with your predilections it would have the reverse ef-fect. Liam still had you, still groped your figure as though it belonged to him, but you'd picked me for the night. Your inconsistency was just the result of working through complicated feelings. You were beginning to unshackle yourself from him.

We finalized our plans for the evening and you went off to Gender and the Consumerist Impulse. On my way back to my room I realized we hadn't discussed what you wanted to write about; I would need to prepare. I rushed over to Sever to catch you, but the class had already begun. The door to the room was open a crack, and I could hear your professor speaking.

It was dicey to loiter outside any classroom for you, especially for a feminism course, where my being caught might itself be fodder for an entire conversation about the male gaze. But there I waited, ears keenly tuned for anything resembling your voice, copy of Emily Dickinson out for pretense and defense. (How could I, a lover of the Amherst recluse, evince any sort of untoward *signifiers*?)

"Cixous's *écriture feminine* is a rebellion against the repressive forces that would silence woman," you said fifteen minutes into class. I leaned in closer to the door. "The verb 'swallowed,' in that passage, is . . . you know." You laughed slightly, and your classmates joined in, in that tepid, tennis-applause way students do when subject matter verges on the bawdy. "It underscores the male's anxiety over his loss of power when woman is allowed to write in her own voice and not in a phallogocentric register."

You contributed two more times with similar eloquence and poise. I'd never heard you speak like this before (had never even heard *woman* used in the singular to represent the plural like that). Our time working on the Henry James paper hadn't revealed anything near this caliber of discourse. Maybe you simply didn't want to do the work for English class and had identified me as a willing and proficient accomplice. Most students didn't have the time to do all the reading for every course.

Or perhaps you were looking for an excuse to spend time with me.

Whatever your reasons, I wasn't upset. I was exultant. You didn't merely appreciate intellect in others; you yourself possessed more brainpower than I'd thought, probably even more than Sara, who had to grind for her grades. You could coast at Harvard on sheer native aptitude. Just like me.

On my walk over to the library I resolved to make this a more intimate meeting than our last study session. I wouldn't let you get away with evasive parries; tonight we would have a real conversation.

When I arrived at our same nook on the second floor, you were already there, punctual for a change, your laptop ready. That boded well.

"Missing a party to work on your essay," I said. "You're turning into a perfect little Harvard student."

"Not missing much," you said.

"I guess there are always plenty of parties to go to, right?"

"I guess."

"I feel like I heard about a big one next weekend in Kirkland."

You didn't say anything. Maybe you'd warm up once we started working.

"Do you know what you want to write on?" I asked.

You reached into your bag, pulled out the course pack for Prufrock, and flipped to "The Yellow Wallpaper." A short story—no wonder you'd read it.

"And what interests you about 'The Yellow Wallpaper'?"

You took a deep breath. "Don't know."

"So you haven't come up with a thesis yet?"

A cute grin. "Maybe you could help me come up with a topic again?"

"I could do that," I said.

You turned the laptop around and pushed it toward me. "How about we connect the narrator's insanity to her desire to write?" I proposed. You nodded, but as soon as I began typing, you pulled back the laptop.

"This is a bad idea," you said, your forehead creasing with worry.

"We can change the thesis if you want. I just came up with that off the top of my head. I didn't really have a chance to prepare."

"No—this." You gesticulated back and forth across the table.

"Why do you say that?"

"I shouldn't be doing this to you." You shut the laptop and pulled it closer. "It's not right."

"You're not doing anything *to* me," I said. "It's *with* me. A big prepositional difference. People work with tutors all the time."

You drummed your fingers on the table. "Not in college."

"Sure they do," I said. "Just think of me like your TF."

"But you're not my TF."

"Technically, no—though Samuelson asked me to take his seminar on Hawthorne next semester, which is mostly grad students," I said. "Not to toot my own horn, but I'm pretty good at this. And there's nothing wrong in asking for help when you need it."

I awaited your response, my calves tensing, the soles of my feet rising as if in high heels.

A sigh of resignation—you knew I was right—and you turned the laptop back to me.

In spite of your ethical reservations, however, once again you didn't contribute at all toward the paper's thesis:

The story implies—perhaps in a manner the author herself was not aware of—that the narrator's desire to write is wedded to her "temporary nervous depression." The hysterical female's creative expression comes at a steep cost: her own mental stability.

"How's that?" I asked after reading it aloud.

"Oops," you said, looking up from your phone. "I was taking care of a text. Can you read it again?"

I repeated myself. "That's really good," you said. "And didn't Samuelson say that Gilman went crazy once she had a kid? So that makes sense that she'd write about a hysterical woman, since she was one herself."

The gulf between how you spoke now and hours earlier in your gender class was remarkable—like a preteen girl here, a seasoned academic there—but I reminded myself that this was a lower-priority course for you. You fielded messages from your buzzing phone while I typed on, feeling as though I'd rescued you from a leaky dinghy and was captaining you to shore in my sturdy vessel.

You listened to a voice mail then made a call, hiding the phone and speaking in a library whisper.

"Mom," you said. "The pharmacy here is out of Ambien. I need you to have Sharon FedEx me a bottle tomorrow." You waited. "*Yes*, I need it tomorrow, you know it's the only way I can fall asleep."

As you talked to her, a shirtless boy ran through the library screaming, "Yale sucks!"

"You going to the Game?" I asked when you were off the phone.

That Saturday was the (football) Game between Harvard and Yale, in all its capitalized and singular hubris (like "the Yard," somewhat like "the city"). I wasn't planning to attend, especially now that I'd been excommunicated by the Matthews Marauders, but it occurred to me that you would likely be there.

"Yeah." You blew your nose on a tissue, and when you set it down a fleck of dried snot protruded from your right nostril like an icicle, shivering in the breeze of your exhalations. I didn't say anything, not only because it's hard to summon the tact to tell anyone, least of all you, she has snot in her nose, but because it was so human, so imperfect.

(See? I didn't just idealize you. I wanted it all: the beauty and the ugliness, the lush hair and the encrusted mucus. Show me someone else who accepted your totality like I did.)

"Cool," I said. "Maybe I'll see you there."

You produced an unconvincing cough. You'd done so at increasingly short intervals for the past twenty minutes, but this time you took it further, moaning and rubbing your temples like an actress in a cold-remedy commercial.

"Fuck," you said. "I think I'm coming down with something."

You sputtered more from your prone position, hacking in a staccato fit but briefly recovering to respond to an incoming text. I'd seen better performances from grade school malingerers.

"I don't know," you said. "I think maybe I better call it a night."

"Okay," I said, snapping your laptop shut.

"Wait—did you send it to yourself?" you asked.

"No, it's your essay. Why would I need to send it to myself?"

"You're not going to . . ." You looked crestfallen. "You can't help me with the rest?"

It was outrageous, asking me to spend the night in the library cheating for you so you could skip off to Liam's party—with you thinking I had no idea what you were up to.

"Yeah, I guess I could."

"Great," you said, smiling with relief. "I'll e-mail you what we have so far." You sent me the document and packed up, leaving me alone in our nook.

Ll'I liam-e uoy tahw ew evah os raf.

I waited a minute before hurrying out of Lamont to catch you in the act.

Ahead of me in the Yard, you turned left through a gate and onto Mass Ave. Yet, instead of going south to Liam's final club (or University Health Services, not that that was ever a consideration), you made a right. You might be meeting him at a bar, in which case I couldn't enter behind you. I kept trailing you anyway, with a wide enough berth that you wouldn't see me even if you happened to look over your shoulder.

After several turns we ended up off campus on Story Street. You stopped at a house and pushed the buzzer. Based on the current information in the student directory, Liam still lived in Adams, and the house didn't appear to be the site of a party; it was quiet, and the only light came from a single third-floor window.

Moments later the front door opened and you stepped inside. I couldn't see who let you in. I prowled closer to see the name under the buzzer to the third floor: MEYERS/BUR, it read, before the cramped handwriting ran out of space.

I walked away, googling "Meyers and Cambridge" but coming up with nothing specific no matter how many Harvard- and address-based modifiers I added. My phone purred with a Facebook notification. You'd posted a photo of me in the library (I hadn't noticed you take it) with the comment "Long night studying at Lamont with **David Federman**." My privacy settings continued to prevent anyone from adding to my own spotless wall. Yet now you were advertising the fact that we were hanging out alone for the whole night. You were even presenting evidence to the world of my writing your essay for you, not that the picture alone could prove it, but you trusted me not to spill our secret. I fiddled with my settings and allowed the picture on my wall, its solitary graphic. Sara had unfriended me and wasn't connected to you—not that I needed to worry about what she thought anymore.

I shouldn't have doubted you. I'd misread the half-written BUR in my haste; it was actually BAR, for "Barrows"—the student directory was erroneous—and Meyers was Liam's roommate. You were sicker than I'd thought and were sleeping it off at his place.

It was odd, though, that you'd posted the photo just now, after we were no longer together.

And suddenly I remembered another surname that began with BUR. I googled "Lucy Meyers." The first hit was the faculty page for a professor of comparative literature at Colby.

Each time Tom Burkhart had been nearby or discussed you seemed so coltish. Those tears, the rapidly responded-to texts, the phone call in the hallway—they had nothing to do with Liam.

And that was why you'd gleefully tagged me on Facebook, to make it appear that you and I hung out (or were "studying") more often than we actually did so that Liam would think you were with innocuous David Federman, not Tom—both now and during the blackout. Maybe you'd used me as an alibi other times, too. I felt cuckolded, strangely, on dim Liam's behalf; you were cheating on both of us. Of all people, Tom—grandstanding, philandering, bearded-and-bespectacled-cliché Tom—shouldn't have been the one who got you.

It made sense, too, why you'd enlisted me to write your essays. Tom was grading them; you wanted to impress him and earn your As, should his postgraduate integrity ever be questioned.

You wouldn't understand, you'd told me, but now I did. I'd make sure you understood, too.

Chapter 13

I completed your essay by Friday afternoon, neglecting my own; it was more important to craft something awe-inspiring to hand in to Tom, that charlatan, who, in heaping hosannas on the paper, would be unwittingly steering you toward the genuinely brilliant scholar in your life. If there's a *Charlotte Perkins Gilman Quarterly* journal out there, I invite its editors to track down those ten and a half pages and publish them. I e-mailed it to you and wrote:

Here you go, ahead of schedule. Hope you're well.

A few hours later you replied:

Thank so much!

No sign-off; not even proper pluralization.

Saturday morning was sunny. Fall had peaked and denuded the trees. My breath fogging in the November chill, I set out for the Game after breakfast, passing over the Charles River on the Anderson Memorial Bridge, from which Quentin Compson leaps to his death in *The Sound and the Fury*, and arrived at the parking lots surrounding Harvard Stadium two hours before the contest kicked off.

I walked through the first passel of tailgates, among the striped tents, the picnic tables decked with buns and condiments, the sibilant grills, the dappled gallery of crimson Harvard and blue Yale sweatshirts, women in stoles lapping up mimosas next to their lock-jawed husbands in coarse black overcoats and wool scarves, students priming kegs and recent graduates nipping from flasks, classic rock guitar solos and hip-hop beats clashing in the air like opposing armies. Two schools equally elite, with imperceptible differences save location, feeding off their insatiable hunger to outrank the other as the Mozart to their Salieri, whose students would have happily attended the rival college had their acceptances and rejections been reversed, which might well have happened had an admissions officer had or not had a sore throat—a headache, eight hours of sleep, horrible commute—the morning their applications were reviewed.

Inside that welter I searched for you, the one person who could make the chaos fade away. I saw the tawny highlights of your hair first, ponytailed and swinging over a black peacoat, poster co-ed from another, more dignified era, as you stood with Suzanne in a mixed-age cluster, all drinking champagne from clear plastic flutes. I crept up behind and waited for an opportunity to catch your attention.

"How's your cold?" I asked when you turned your head to blow out smoke.

Your expression was hidden by oversized sunglasses. "Much better," you said in a raspy voice, tapping your cigarette to dislodge a glowing clump of ash. "See ya," you added, ready to return to your crew.

"I know where you went the other night," I said softly, so the others couldn't hear. "After Lamont."

"I don't know what you're talking about," you said after a few seconds, also quietly, but the delay and volume betrayed the claim.

"Tom," I mouthed.

Your sunglasses fixed me in a lengthy, hard stare. Then you ushered me in the direction of the cooler.

"You went to his place on Story Street," I said once we were far enough from the others.

"You *followed* me?"

"There are no rules against walking around the streets," I said. "But it *is* against university policy for a grad student to be with an undergrad he's teaching. It's considered sexual harassment, even if it's consensual."

You swallowed some champagne.

"And I assume you know he's married."

"I'm aware," you said with a mirthless laugh.

"I just don't want to see you get hurt. He's not going to leave his wife for you, if that's what you're expecting."

"Thanks for the concern, David." You smiled sarcastically and turned to go back to your people.

I reached out and tapped your back. "You should report what happened to the Ad Board."

You whipped around.

"If you're scared, you can bring me along as a personal advisor and I can do most of the talking," I offered. "I researched how it's done. They'll just need you to corroborate. You won't get in any trouble, only him. No one else will even find out." I sounded unusually confident, in charge, as if I made it a regular habit to save beautiful women from themselves.

You gave me another long look, but this time your mouth softened. Resting a hand on my shoulder, you shook your head. "Thank you, but don't worry about me. I was about to break things off anyway."

"You were?"

"Yeah." You exhaled smoke with a rueful scowl.

"So you'll go to the Ad Board?"

"I would. Except you know how these things always work out. Even if the guy gets punished, the girl gets shamed for it," you said. "Sorry about my reaction before. I appreciate you looking out for me. Obviously, this is not something I want other people to know about. I hope I can trust you, David."

"Of course," I said, trying not to smile. I'd done it: Liam had never been the real competitor; Tom was, and now I'd knocked him, if not out of the school, then out of contention.

"How's that champagne?" I asked as you started to walk back to the others.

You paused, trying to come up with a witty line for me. "It makes being around the alumni tolerable."

"So getting drunk is a prerequisite for hanging out here?" I grabbed one of the open bottles submerged in a cooler of ice and a flute from a stack.

You shrugged. I poured myself a serving and took a cold, fizzy draft.

"You're right," I said. "It's already making them better."

Suzanne drifted over, looking at her phone. "Jen's still in bed with a hangover," she reported. "She said she wishes we'd gotten her stomach pumped last night. And she left her credit card at the bar."

"Hi, again," I said. "Famous David."

Suzanne glanced at you. "The man who needs no introduction."

As the two of you recapped Jen's wild antics the previous night, one of the older men came along and inserted himself into our trio. He wore a corduroy baseball cap emblazoned with an *H*, the end of its adjustable strap dangling like a vestigial tail.

"You kids having fun?" he asked with the bluster of a host proud to have comely young women he didn't know at his party.

"Absolutely," said Suzanne.

"Go Harvard," he cheered, making a small fist. Suzanne mimicked him with a smile.

"Beat Yale," you said.

"That's what I like to see," said the man. "Good old-fashioned school spirit."

"Destroy them," you added.

"Our guys have looked good this year," he said.

"Dismember them and send them back to New Haven in body bags." You beamed at him as if you'd said something adorable. I felt the first pinpricks of an erection, ogling the scar on your forehead, a seam into your skull, wishing I could open it up, rappel inside, and suture it back together so I could swim around your brain undisturbed.

The man chuckled. "Well," he said with a diplomatic smile he'd doubtless used in hundreds of hostile boardrooms, "you kids have fun."

After he found shelter with a safer set of people, Suzanne cackled. "Cheeky," she said. "Always biting the hand that feeds you."

Marco Lazzarini, the aristocratic Italian among your friends, swanned over, talking about his upcoming trip to Barcelona. For the remainder of the tailgate I hovered by your side (maybe I hadn't been overtly invited at first, but you weren't going to evict me now), maintained a steady intake of champagne, and celebrated Thanksgiving early with gratitude that I wasn't trapped with Sara and the Marauders. How dispensable are most people in our lives, collections of matter filling empty space until they're recycled.

Throughout all this a cavalcade of males of varying ages found excuses to sidle up and talk to you and Suzanne—mostly you. Though you treated them with more civility than you had the patron of our party, you weren't letting them into our circle, and inevitably they backed off. Their unabashed attempts to court your attention amused me. I didn't need to do a pathetic song and dance for you. I was the one you trusted.

When the tailgates closed down at kickoff the three of us mo-
seyed back over the Anderson Memorial Bridge (Justin and Kevin
would have approved of our pregaming without going to the actual
game). You led us to a final club—not Liam's—where we rolled liquor around our mouths and sampled hors d'oeuvres of deviled eggs,
sashimi, and goat cheese croquettes among an intergenerational
assembly of alumni before progressing to a different establishment,
the sun-slanted afternoon pushed away by gray early evening, which
surrendered to inky night, hours and hours with you, eventually
ending up, to my dismay, at the club of your school-sanctioned boyfriend.

Yet Liam was nowhere to be seen. I tried to piece together why
you'd remained with him through your affair. Perhaps it was so that
you wouldn't feel as though you were just the other woman, desperately pining after a taken man, and had kept him around to make
Tom jealous. Or maybe it was for whatever social status he supplied
you with that Tom couldn't because your relationship had been illicit.

You and Suzanne colonized the same sofa as before and I sat
next to you, no longer banished to the armrest. Cole Porter lyrics
crooned over the sound system as grandfatherly benefactors limped
about. Harvard had lost the game, demoralizing the fan base and
further buoying my own spirits; I'd been dreading the mass celebra-
tory atmosphere, the drunken woo-hoos in the streets, the spoils
of war that would all redound to the benefit of the gridiron heroes
(glory, fellatio). Now the victory parade was only for me.

My phone trembled in my pocket. A text from Sara:

I found one of your Lactaid pills under my bed today. Dot dot
dot.

I didn't respond. She sent another message fifteen minutes later:

(Subtext: Thinking of you.)

A twenty-something alumnus, vice president of moving money from one account to another, insinuated himself into our space and hit on you, directing an occasional word to Suzanne out of politesse. "I have to meet some friends at the Charles," he said. "You should come."

His canvas belt was embroidered with little anchors and sailboats. I remembered a childhood story about a classmate's uncle who had been garroted by a taut cord while sailing, and cast the alum in my mental reenactment.

"Thanks, but we're good here for now," you said.

"We'll be at the bar late. Stop by whenever." He winked. "I'm staying there, room 201."

"God, I should write my essay on the *alumni*," Suzanne said after he left. "They're even worse than the current members."

"What's the essay for?" I asked, eager to guide the conversation toward my bailiwick.

Suzanne hesitated.

"Can we *not* talk about school right now?" you cut in. "We're almost on vacation."

"Duly noted," Suzanne said. "Who needs a refill?"

She went to the bar. "Do you have any special plans for Thanksgiving?" I asked you.

"Just hanging at home with good ol' Larry and Margaret."

"That should be relaxing."

You expelled air between your tongue and palate, generating a cynical *t* sound. "Gag me."

"I know," I said, *gag em*. When Suzanne returned you made more space for her, our pelvises making unbroken if involuntary contact on the crammed sofa, how quaint that you had once touched your elbow to mine in class and now we were almost literally joined at the hip. The two of you resumed talking as I fantasized about the future with you: champagne and sashimi and sofas but, more important, the thrill of savoring these things by your side, the ecstatic rush of being alive, right here, right this moment, that had so rarely visited me in my lifetime of safely plodding preparation for the future.

Liam appeared, ruiner of everything good.

"Veronica," he commanded in his uncouth baritone. Just that one word, as if you were a pet. I could provoke a breakup by informing him of what had been going on with Tom through a pseudonymous e-mail, but I was one of a select few—if not the only person—who knew, and you would figure out I was the source. You might end things on your own anyway, especially under the influence of your gender class; you knew he was a repressive force who sought to silence you. And yet that was what apparently attracted you to him.

"What's up, Suzanne?" Liam said, planting himself between the two of you on the couch. He reached over to the antipasto board occupying the coffee table where we had previously snorted cocaine. Slicing a thick coin of sausage, he popped it into his mouth as if he were a meat grinder.

"How were the other clubs?" He gnashed the red meat between his teeth and cut another piece of sausage.

"They were lame, but they had—" Your eyes bulged with alarm. "You're *bleeding*."

He'd nicked his index finger with the knife and blood was leaking out.

"Oh," he said lunkheadedly. "Whatever."

You took a cocktail napkin from the table and wrapped it around his finger. "*Baby*, you have to be more careful," you cooed with a tenderness I had no idea you possessed.

It was all an act. You were exaggerating your caretaking so he wouldn't suspect you of infidelity.

"Liam, you know David," you said.

He looked at me. "David from English," he said. "David from Lamont."

"Yep," I said, afraid of making eye contact with either of you, even though I was in a position of power, knowing all about a situation of which he was completely ignorant.

"So you guys pulled an all-nighter?"

Detecting a note of unease in Liam's voice, I waited a beat before answering, hoping to preserve your impression of me as a trustworthy ally while simultaneously arousing his suspicion. "Yeah, it was a really late night."

"And Thursday night, too?"

"Uh-huh," I said. (I'd spent that night overhearing Steven practice his magic act.)

"Enough with the cross-examination," you interrupted. "Yes, we worked until very late both nights. Jesus."

"I'm just making conversation," he said innocently. He turned to me. "She's always saying I don't engage her friends enough."

"You're being a dick," you hissed.

A crocodile grin spread over his face. "You're so cute when you're angry." He squeezed your pouting cheeks together with his uninjured hand.

"Fuck off," you said, pushing him away. "I'm going home. The alumni here make me sick." You stood up and put on your coat.

"She'll be fine," Liam announced as the three of us watched you stomp off. He carved himself another piece of sausage before joining his friends by the pool table.

"And the fun never ends," Suzanne said, leaving for the bar.

I caught up to you again on Mt. Auburn Street.

"What do you want?" you snapped as I matched your stride.

"Nothing," I said. "Just heading back, too. You *are* going to Matthews, right?"

After entering our dorm you sped upstairs ahead of me, not pausing to say good-bye at the fourth-floor landing. You hadn't even thanked me in person for the second essay. In a few days you'd be back in New York. All the momentum I'd built up would be lost.

The dorm was quiet, everyone out at one of the Harvard-Yale parties. I went to my room and wrote you an e-mail:

It's polite to say good night to someone. Especially someone who's done a lot of favors for you and is looking out for your best interests.

A few minutes passed. You didn't reply. I followed up with a stronger message:

P.S. I've been thinking it over. TB abused his power and he'll continue doing it, if not with you, then someone else. I'm emailing the Ad Board now. It's the right thing to do.

I was composing a third e-mail—a draft of the letter that I would threaten to send to the Ad Board—when the knock came. I carried my laptop with me as I opened the door.

"David, it's really not a good idea to get mixed up in this," you said, the hallway light haloing your hair.

"Guys like him always think they can get away with stuff like this," I said. "Someone needs to stop him."

A girl walked down the hall. You waited until she passed.

"He won't do it with anyone else," you said quietly.

"If this were a friend of yours, you'd do what I'm doing," I said in a normal voice. "You're scared, you feel like you've done something wrong, but you haven't. He's exploited you with his position. You're the victim here."

I returned to my desk and set my laptop down as if I were about to fire off the career-ending missive. You followed me in and shut the door behind you.

"I should be the one to do it, then." You pushed the laptop closed and kept your hand pressed on top of it.

"You'll talk to the Ad Board?"

You nodded.

"Do you have hard evidence?" I asked. "E-mails?"

"He never put anything incriminating in e-mail."

"You must have texts with him," I said. "Even if he deletes his, you still have them on your phone."

You shook your head. "He uses a prepaid phone so his wife won't see; he could deny writing them. My testimony is the only way to do it."

"Do you want me to be there with you when you end things with him?"

"No," you said. "He's not dangerous. Just an asshole."

Your eyes landed on the framed photo atop the bookcase of Steven and his cheerful parents on vacation in some warm-weather climate. You picked it up and studied it.

"Maybe you should try being with a nice guy for a change," I said. "Or at least an assholish nice guy."

The room's silence was pierced by some stray shouts from the Yard.

"Maybe," you said a little shyly, at last acknowledging what was getting harder to ignore the past few weeks. I thought of when I stood outside Sara's door, timidly paging through *101 Idealistic Jobs That Actually Exist*, how all I'd had to do was act the way I knew she wanted me to.

I leaned forward to kiss you. You recoiled.

"What the hell?" My tone and volume surprised us both. You held the picture frame up in front of you as if for protection.

"What's your fucking problem?" I felt myself becoming hard. "You think I'm not good enough for you?"

"There's no problem," you said softly.

"Then put the picture down," I ordered, just the way Liam bossed you around. As I advanced forward a step, you took one back.

"There's no problem," you repeated, finding yourself against the wall. Your hands dropped slowly but continued to clutch the photo. When I attempted to pry it from your fingers, you pushed my hand aside and gently pressed the long side of the frame against my crotch.

"This feels good, doesn't it," you said, running the frame up and down.

"Yes," I said. "But put the picture down."

"Shh." You clamped your hand over my mouth. "Do you want me to keep going?"

I made an affirmative guttural sound as the Zengers merrily grooved over my stiff penis. I closed my eyes and you slid the picture faster and faster, buffing the surface, the friction heating up the denim, the bodily sensation less titillating than the psychological one, the first tremors of orgasm announcing themselves before the seismic wave.

"You really *are* an asshole," you whispered in my ear, and I exploded, my legs buckling from the release of tension, hands groping the desk for support, a wail of the deepest rapture rising from my throat as you withdrew your hand from my face.

Then it was over and you were halfway out the door. I watched you go, collapsing into my desk chair like a boxer onto his corner stool after a twelve-round match.

It was happening.

Chapter 14

I didn't see you in the dining hall the next day, or the day after that. I could have e-mailed you, but I wanted to let things run their natural course. Our breakthrough would propel us to the subsequent, inevitable phase.

The night before the penultimate Prufrock I stayed up until sunrise writing my own paper, "I'm Nobody! Who Are You?: The Self as Staffage in Emily Dickinson." I printed a copy for my section leader, then saved her the trouble of passing it along to Samuelson by e-mailing it to him directly. More public accolades for my work in front of you couldn't hurt.

There were two possible explanations for your absence in class: you'd gone home early for Thanksgiving break or you were avoiding Tom. (Perhaps the Ad Board had advised you to do so as they prepared to bring formal charges against him.) He looked so pleased to be him, finger combing his wavy locks, stretching his arms up as he yawned, leaping to his feet and making a show of holding the door for the girl who arrived on crutches. The darling of the Harvard English department, who cowardly skirted loneliness when his pretty professor wife was away by taking advantage of the school's most beautiful (and, fortuitously for him, emotionally masochistic) undergrad. He had no idea what was coming, the dolt. Life's delicacies had been served to him on a platter, he'd devoured far more than his fair share, and now they were about to be whisked away.

The day before Thanksgiving I took the T to South Station and boarded an overheated, full-capacity Greyhound reeking of fast food and body odor. Five hours later I debussed in Newark, New Jersey, where my mother was waiting to pick me up. As I climbed into the passenger seat, she leaned across the console to give me a seat-belt-restrained embrace. "Welcome home!" she said.

In the beginning of the semester, when classmates had asked where I was from, their eyes lit up at the first word—a *New Yorker*, you could see them thinking—as I dithered before arriving at the letdown of the second. Ah, just a dime-a-dozen Jersey boy, punch line of America, our only selling points tomatoes and a blue-collar troubadour who had named one of his best albums after Nebraska.

And I couldn't even claim affiliation with the plucky working-class Joisey of Springsteen lyrics. My milieu was that of the fairly successful professionals who weren't quite able to hack it across the river and so had settled for suburban convenience, good public schools, and affordable real estate while living in the shadows of glittering skyscrapers.

On the ride home my mother asked about my courses and friends, and I told the truth about the former and succinct lies about the latter. I didn't reveal that my second-class citizenship in the Matthews Marauders had vaporized because I'd broken up with my she-seems-nice girlfriend, whom I'd dated primarily to gain access to her roommate, a semester-long odyssey, a girl with whom I had (thanks to my essay-writing abilities and compromised academic morality, along with her angst over her self-destructive romantic entanglements) partaken in denim-mediated ménage à Zengers— oh, speaking of sexualized clothing materials, for onanistic activity I also purloined the girl's bathrobe belt, the tip of which lives in my pocket, and I may as well mention that I've gotten into this kind of porn where the woman belittles the viewer about his inadequate manhood—but, yeah, classes are going swell and I'm having a blast, how're Dad and Anna and Miriam?

After dinner, to avoid my older sister and her abrasively out-going boyfriend, I hid in our finished basement to watch TV. The boyfriend came downstairs anyway while I was flipping channels, so I stayed on a revisionist documentary about Christopher Colum-bus in hopes of boring him off. A self-proclaimed "Columbus buff," he happily settled in. As I stood by the basement fridge, nibbling at a fruit platter intended for Thanksgiving, my phone dinged with an e-mail from Daniel Hallman about an unofficial high school re-union he'd gotten wind of that was happening RIGHT NOW at Ap-plebee's (the one at the mall). A few weeks ago I would have deleted it immediately. But I'd had sex now, twice. And been brought to or-gasm by you. No one at Hobart High had ever seen *this* David Fed-erman. They hadn't really been acquainted with the first iteration, either—but that was just as well.

I borrowed my mother's car and drove past the gated condo-minium communities and the gargantuan houses that looked like they'd just had cellophane peeled off them, their driveways full of SUVs and hockey nets, the lawns cleared of leaves, and arrived at the mall. An immaculately mopped retail complex with a cornuco-pia of national franchises to suit one's every consumerist impulse: there was the Cheesecake Factory, where I'd celebrated my sixteenth birthday with my family; Foot Locker, purveyor of all my white

sneakers; the Gap, my annual back-to-school jeans and shirts mer-
chant; and Panda Express and Perfumania, Vitamin World and Vic-
toria's Secret, Abercrombie & Fitch and American Eagle, their logos
as familiar as national landmarks.

And there was Applebee's. (Why, I thought, is an Applebee's
not a s'eebelppA, nor, for that matter, an Orangebird's?) My former classmates milled about within expected spheres. I walked past
the popular kids near the front, Paul de Witt and Joel Blum and
Laurel Wilcox-Richards and Heidi McMasters and their respective
aides-de-camp. There wasn't a single greeting from them, not even
a nod of recognition. I could've been a busboy clearing away their
popcorn shrimp. That was fine; they seemed so provincial now, attending their respectable second-tier institutions, continuing their
alcohol and pot habits at frat parties with bourgeois predictability
while, unbeknownst to them, I was doing coke at a Harvard final
club.

"ID?" the bartender asked when I ordered a vodka soda.

"Shit," I said, digging through my wallet. "I must have left it at
college."

Root beer in hand, I located my erstwhile clique, or three-fifths
of it. (No one had heard from Michael Lu since he'd left for the University of Chicago.) The attention was on Daniel, who was catalogu-
ing his adventures with blackouts and six-packs, bongs and sluts. He
bragged about his hookup tally: a baker's dozen so far this semester
at Wisconsin, a number so outlandish that he couldn't have been
making it up. It took them all a moment to realize I was there and,
after a round of hellos, Daniel picked up where he'd left off, breaking
out his phone to show us pictures of three conquests on Facebook
(surely the better-looking ones).

He polled the others on how they had fared in that department.
Unwillingly celibate Paresh deflected and stammered. Perspiring
like a criminal under the interrogation lights, George claimed to
have gotten two blow jobs.

"What about you, David?" Daniel asked with the cocksureness of being the sexual lieutenant of our blundering platoon. "You tap any Harvard ass yet?"

I hadn't wanted to cheapen our experience by citing it in present company, but Daniel posed the question with such slick hostility that I couldn't resist. "A couple," I said.

"A couple," he repeated. "Meaning you were with a couple, like in a threesome, so now you're bisexual?"

Titters from Paresh and George.

"Here's one," I said, pulling up your Facebook profile on my phone. Their greasy fingers passed you and your plaid shirt around.

"She's hot," Paresh said.

"Superhot," seconded George.

"You're boning *her*?" Daniel asked, incredulous.

"Ask me at Christmas break."

"What does that mean?"

"It's only a matter of time," I said coolly. "On Saturday night she gave me a hand job."

"Ooh, a *hand job*." He snickered. "What is this, the eighth-grade trip to Washington, DC?"

"I'm taking it slow," I said, regretting the disclosure. "She's not the kind of girl who's just another notch on your bedpost. This is serious."

"If you're not fucking, exactly what kind of 'serious' things do you do with her?"

"We go to parties at final clubs. Sometimes we do coke."

"Coca-Cola," George said, looking at Daniel for approval while hyperventilating with laughter.

"If you're really hooking up with her, text her something," Daniel challenged me.

"She's with her family. I don't want to bother her."

Daniel folded his arms and grinned at the others. "He doesn't even have her number. Because he's *taking it slow*."

"Fine," I said. "I'll e-mail her. This is so stupid. I'm sure she's out in Manhattan now. She lives on the Upper East Side."

I said the last two sentences looking down at my phone, knowing without seeing their faces that they were impressed. As they bunched around the screen, I composed a Facebook message:

At high school reunion. Gag me. How is your vacation going?

I pocketed the phone and kept my hand on it in case it vibrated.

Daniel went to the bathroom and, on the return trip, with his crudely acquired sexual bravado, somehow managed to wangle a conversation with Heidi McMasters. Daniel Hallman talking to Heidi McMasters! It would have been inconceivable six months ago. As Paresh and George compared the merits of their school's dormitories, I watched Daniel feign suaveness. My initial envy was tempered by seeing Heidi, for the first time, for what she was: just a cute suburban girl whose best years were already behind her. He strode back to us as if nothing out of the ordinary had happened, deliberately not mentioning his transcendence of previously impermeable social borders so that Paresh and George would obsequiously grill him, the intrepid explorer, about the otherworldly wonders he'd glimpsed in his travels.

As the night ended, Daniel asked if my "hand-job queen" had written back.

"No," I said. "I remembered she was going to see a movie tonight."

"Do you even really know this girl?" he taunted. "Or do you just jerk off to her picture?"

"Of course I know her," I said. "I see her all the time." The only photo of us actually together also included Sara, with my arm around her, and if it came out that I'd been dating her, they'd never believe I had also hooked up with you. And the one of me at the library would provide Daniel with more ammunition—that you must have been giving me hand jobs under the table all night long while we studied.

Maybe you really were at a movie. Even so, there was no need for you to ignore me, not after what we'd done together. It was less than a week ago, but the memory was already growing fuzzy. Talking about you in the third person almost made me feel as if I'd conjured you up, a character in a dream. It'd all be better once school resumed and I saw you again. But four days was too long to wait.

After logging another sixty hours with the Federmans, on Saturday morning I told my mother I'd made plans to meet a college friend in Manhattan and would she mind dropping me off at the train station after lunch?

"Of course," she answered, and asked when I'd be back.

"I'm not sure," I said. "If it's late, I'll take a taxi home from the station." Then, optimistically: "I may just sleep over and come back in the morning. Okay if I play it by ear?"

Most eighteen-year-olds in my position might have had to negotiate to stay out late in New York City without concrete expectation of a return. My mother couldn't have looked more pleased I was getting out of the house. Chumless David, who'd spent his adolescence in his room, who hadn't had so much as a sleepover past the age of nine, had not only made a close friend at school, but a Manhattan sophisticate to boot.

"Perfectly fine," she said.

"Are you kidding me?" Anna whined. "You wouldn't let me see Sophie tonight because you said we *all* have go to the Goldmans'. Why is *he* allowed to get out of it?"

"David's in college," my mother told her. "He's allowed to visit his friend in the city if he wants."

Before leaving I mapped out which subway to take down to Zipper & Button, the clothing boutique in SoHo whose label was on your black sweater. Riding the A train, my reflection in the window that of a disgruntled native, I thought of taking a selfie and sending it to Daniel Hallman, telling him I was clothes shopping in downtown Manhattan today; did he want me to pick up anything for him, or did he prefer to stick to the mall?

The streets were clogged with shoppers chasing post-Thanksgiving sales. Zipper & Button, however, advertised no holiday deals and was empty but for two unsmiling female clerks. They looked up from their conspiratorial huddle behind the counter and gave me a cold, cursory appraisal.

With its exposed-brick walls and creaky floors, the space felt more like someone's home than a store. From speakers whispered an acoustic guitar and a woman singing in what sounded like a Scandinavian dialect. Inventory was sparse and didn't look particularly masculine. It occurred to me this might be a women's-only shop.

I took another lap around the racks to check that I hadn't missed anything. This time I located a sweater identical to the one you wore, two lines of stitching from the shoulders meeting at the chest, only in gray instead of black. I brought it to the counter.

"Is this men's?" I asked.

"Unisex," they answered together. *Xesinu.*

I took it into the dressing stall and pulled it over my T-shirt. It softly conformed to my upper body, a luxurious departure from the lumpy, scratchy sweaters of unwanted childhood gifts. Next to my Gap jeans and Foot Locker sneakers, it looked incongruous, the brooding musician whose siblings were a dentist and a database administrator. I needed a whole new wardrobe, but this was a start. *For the price I'm paying,* I heard my father grumble, *you'd think they could throw in a pair of pants.*

I charged the sweater to my debit card, wore it out of the store, hopped on the uptown 6 train, and walked over to Park Avenue, where I found the elegant prewar residence of good ol' Larry and Margaret.

My plan was to sit in a restaurant or coffee shop with a view of your building. At some point you'd pop out for a cigarette, and that's when our coincidental run-in would transpire. I'd dart out and we'd laughingly exchange *What are* you *doing here?*s. *Oh, I just saw a friend, but I have a few hours to kill before my train; sure, I could join you for a walk through Central Park.* Away from school, away from Tom and Liam and Suzanne and Jen and Christopher and Andy and everyone else, you could be your unguarded self. *Don't take the train back,* you would plead as dusk descended. *Stay here, my parents are dying to meet you.* You'd bring me back to your apartment, feverish with excitement. *So this is the David we've been hearing so much about!* Margaret would swoon.

But during my many jaunts down your block through Google Street View, I'd failed to notice the critical oversight in my strategy: Park was strictly residential. There wasn't a single commercial establishment that could serve as an inconspicuous hideout; it was as if the avenue were designed to discourage the casual lurker.

A landscaped meridian bisected north- and southbound lanes of traffic, with concrete embankments serving as islands for pedestrians who didn't catch the green light in time to make it all the way across the boulevard. Raised flower beds bordered interior strips of each median that had held grass in warmer months.

I stood in the middle of the crosswalk opposite your building, surveying my options. If I waited on the sidewalk right outside your home, I would blow my cover; if you saw me sitting on the edge of the island's empty flower bed, you'd know I was on a stakeout. Failing to come up with a better solution, I decided to stay put. Under the pretense of waiting to cross the street, I remained adrift on my concrete no-man's-land, eyes fixed on the green awning that canopied a set of double doors from which you might at any point emerge.

As the afternoon sun sank, suffusing the street with a tangerine glow, the indigenous species of the Upper East Side meandered by, women with pinched faces and coiffed hair, their toy dogs snug in cashmere sweaters, nonagenarians escorted by uniformed help, teens in sweatpants with the names of their prep schools scrolled in oversized fonts down the legs, towheaded toddlers slumbering in strollers.

Your building's doorman, dressed in a brass-buttoned suit and a porter's hat, maintained equal vigilance from his post inside your lobby so as not to be caught unawares by an approaching resident. And he never was, always anticipating the precise moment to turn the handle and swing the door open, stepping aside and acknowledging the occupant's return with a deferential nod.

Every so often the door would open and he'd march out on his own to the curb, blow a whistle, and wave a white-gloved hand at the oncoming traffic. A yellow cab would screech to a stop in front of the awning and a resident would materialize from the lobby and climb in.

After one of these excursions, rather than going back inside the building, he headed over to my island. I typed pointlessly into my phone.

"You waiting for someone?" he asked in a gruff outer-borough accent.

"I'm doing a study on pedestrian traffic for Harvard University," I told him. "I'm measuring the ebb and flow of population density and calculating carrying capacity."

I held up my phone, ostensible proof of my scientific method.

"Harvard?" He grimaced, looked around as if uncertain what to do with this information, and nodded. "All right."

Evening set in. The temperature dropped and it began drizzling. I thought about running over to another avenue to buy an umbrella, but if you chose that interval for your appearance, all my work would have been for naught.

The sky cleaved and the drizzle turned into a downpour. The only awning nearby was your own, and I couldn't make that my haven. All I could do was stay in place, getting soaked as walkers scattered and I remained the one person outside sans umbrella.

On top of being wet, I was hungry, cold, and tired from standing. I didn't know if you were home; if so, when you'd be leaving; or, if you were out, when you'd be returning. Yet the adverse conditions only fortified my determination. I was scaling Everest. It'd be another heroic story to tell you someday.

As it turned out, you were home.

You carried an open umbrella out of the lobby around ten o'clock, walked to the corner opposite where I stood, and stepped off the curb. My fatigued quadriceps contracted with anticipation. I stayed where I was, assuming you were going to cross the street in my direction, but instead you held up your hand to hail a taxi, forgoing your doorman's services.

"Hey!" I yelled, but my voice was lost in the thrum of raindrops and whistling traffic. Two cabs spotted you simultaneously and jockeyed for your fare at the corner. While you folded your umbrella and climbed into the nearest one, I made a cavalier dash across the street. Your car took off as I jumped into the second cab, my wet jeans squeaking against the pleather seat.

"Follow that cab directly in front of us," I told the driver. "Please."

A chase sequence in traffic-jammed Manhattan wasn't as exhilarating as it might sound. We stopped at frequent red lights; our cars never exceeded fifteen miles per hour; my driver yammered on the phone the whole time in a foreign language.

When we reached your destination, the rain had stopped. Our cabs pulled up in tandem at a curb that, according to the on-screen map, was on the Lower East Side. I paid with my debit card but had trouble swiping it cleanly, and by the time I was done you'd disappeared into a bar on the corner. A squat man with an imperious stomach guarded the door. I could wait until you departed, but at that point you might be headed home. And I was tired of waiting.

I sauntered up to the bar's entrance, scratching the back of my neck and checking my phone with blasé distraction. Slouched on a stool, hands in the pockets of a puffy jacket, the bouncer barely lifted his eyes from his own phone. "ID," he mumbled.

"I left my wallet here last night," I said. "They're expecting me."

He yawned and blinked wearily. "Can't let you in without ID."

"My friend got his stomach pumped because he was here last night," I said. "We had to leave right away, and I've been in the hospital with him all night and day. I've got a flight tomorrow, and if I don't get it—"

He released a bored sigh. "Make it quick," he said.

My first time in a bar—and a New York City bar, at that. But it wasn't what I had expected from a Manhattan establishment, nor was it the kind of place I would've guessed you'd haunt. Bad eighties music shrieked on a jukebox; retro arcade games blinked and blipped against one wall; the floor was sticky with beer. A number of ironic moustaches and earnest beards among the male clientele; the women seemed intent on marring their looks with conscientiously frumpy clothes and eccentric glasses.

I pretzeled into an opening at the bar, but the bartender kept fielding orders from whoever was next to me. After the third such slight, I managed to interpose a request. She cupped her hand behind her ear.

I held up two fingers. "Vod-ka so-das!" I hollered, and scanned the crowd for you while I waited. There was another room in the back. You had to be there.

The bartender served me my drinks and asked if I wanted to start a tab. Low on cash, I said yes and gave her my debit card. I chugged one of the drinks and took the other to the back room, shaky from the booze on an empty stomach and a day of standing guard in the rain.

And there you were. Yes—that was your head; I could pick out that compound of colors in the stands of a stadium. You sat on a stool at the corner of a high-top table with two girls, your back to me. I bushwhacked through a thicket of twenty-somethings, the last leg of a grueling obstacle course. The day had worn me down, but I suddenly felt helium-filled, it had all been worth it, who cared if I woke up with a cold tomorrow. I stifled a keyed-up laugh as I reached out to tap your shoulder. You twisted around and the scar on your forehead shot up in surprise.

"I *thought* that was you!" I said. "Funny bumping into you like this."

You glanced at your two companions before looking back at me.

"So, how was your Thanksgiving with good ol' Larry and Margaret?" I asked.

"It was fine." You fingered the straw in your drink. "How'd you know their names?"

"It came up the last time we hung out, after the Harvard-Yale Game," I said. "You were pretty inebriated," I added chucklingly, to explain your forgetfulness to the two other girls.

You squinted at me before responding. "What are you doing here?"

"Meeting up with some old friends," I said. "I'm early."

You took a long sip.

"Did you get a chance to"—sotto voce, though the other girls were now talking among themselves—"talk to the Ad Board?"

The straw still in your mouth, eyes on mine, you nodded once.

"Good," I said. "You've done the right thing."

"Where d'you get that sweater?" you asked. (Where'd *Jew* get that sweater, it sounded like.)

I looked down as if to remind myself of what sweater I'd worn that day. "Christmas," I said. "I got it for Christmas last year."

"Veronica, who's your friend?" one of the girls you were with cut in.

"This is David," you said. "He goes to school with me."

The friend translated for the third girl, who couldn't hear. "From Harvard!" she shouted.

"We're in the same dorm," you said.

"I used to date her roommate," I clarified, bellying up to the table.

You stood up and offered me your seat. "We were actually just about to leave, if you want to claim this table for when your friends get here."

"Thanks," I said. "But they won't be here for a bit. You guys should stay another round."

"Unfortunately, we really have to go." You buttoned your coat. "It was great running into you."

"Stay for one more," I said. "It's on me. I insist." I leaned over the table and made eye contact with your friends. "What are you guys drinking?"

"Scotch and soda," one answered.

"Gin martini, extra dirty," requested the other.

I looked at you. "I'm good." You sat back down.

"I'll get you a vodka soda, just in case," I said, tapping the table as I left.

Back in the other room, it again took a while to get the bartender's attention. "Close out your tab or keep it open?" she asked.

"Keep it open," I told her. "The night's just beginning."

Four drinks was too many to carry in one trip, so I guzzled my own and cradled the other three against my chest as I began the perilous journey back, bracing for impact from rogue elbows, from men stepping back for full-bodied laughter, from women's swinging bags.

When I arrived at the table your stools were empty. You must have gone to the bathroom together, as girls are wont to do. Better to stay there, I reasoned, than wander around the bar and lose you.

Ten minutes later I took out my phone and wrote you a message on Facebook:

Got the drinks. Where are you?

"Sorry, these seats are occupied," I told a party of women who attempted to take your stools.

After a few minutes, when you still hadn't shown, I surrendered the table to the glaring women and relocated your drinks to a ledge on a nearby wall, in unfortunate proximity to a speaker. "Sweet Caroline" came on, to cheers from the patrons. I wrote you again:

I had to give up the stools and moved to a wall.

I started sipping the scotch and soda.

The wall with an exit sign.

The densely packed room and the alcohol and the long day and my waterlogged clothes coalesced in a queasy, moist heat. "*So good! So good! So good!*" a man bellowed in my ear.

You probably didn't receive Facebook notifications on your phone; that would account for why you hadn't responded to the one I sent from Applebee's. I wrote you at your Harvard e-mail:

In case you didn't get my Facebook messages am with our drinks against the wall with the exit sign.

I polished off the martini. Your vodka soda I refused to besmirch with my lips and carried with me as I made my way to the front room, digging a thumb inside my jeans pocket and rubbing the piece of your belt. The stitched initials gave the weightless silk a feeling of tangibility, of something that could be held and corralled.

You'd ditched me.

My attempt to blunt my anger by drinking your vodka soda was a mistake. Vision juddering, a medley of liquors roiling inside me, I lumbered to the men's room. I made it just in time, barging into the graffiti-tagged stall and kneeling in front of the scummy toilet seconds before my body rejected the poison. I cleaned myself up, hailed a cab back to Penn Station, remembered I'd left my card at the bar, apologized profusely as I handed the driver my remaining cash, and missed the last train by three minutes.

A cab to New Jersey would be exorbitant, and I'd have to wake my parents up and ask them to come downstairs and pay for it, with me drunk and disheveled. My return ticket granted me the privilege of staying overnight in the station. I sat against a wall, not letting myself nod off for fear of the indigent drifters who were also taking refuge there, waves of rage and nausea cresting in alternation, the swelling of one temporarily abating the other. As I scrutinized your Facebook page for any hints of where you'd gone, my phone died, leaving me with nothing but my acid thoughts for five hours.

I took the first train in the morning and walked an hour home from the station. "Taking a nap before my bus," I called to my parents in the kitchen.

"Sounds like someone had a big night out in the city," my mother said.

I got in bed, plugging in my phone and checking my e-mail. One new message, sent a few hours after my phone had died.

Just got email. Friend had emergency. Had to leave.

I responded:

No problem! I gave your drinks to my friends. We had a fun night. Hope your friend's okay.

I nestled into my pillow but, despite my exhaustion, couldn't fall asleep, buzzed on the welcome relief of knowing you hadn't intentionally abandoned me, even feeling a little foolish for my premature, unwarranted fury. Of course there'd been a reason.

Chapter 15

Following Thanksgiving vacation, we had a truncated week of classes, then reading period, then exams. I showed up early to the final lecture of Prufrock. Tom was at his usual post near the back. Had you not gone to the Ad Board as you'd claimed? No; he was either still unaware of the imminent charges or in denial, assuming it would blow over.

Further confirming this, you were already there for once, in the front row, to keep your distance from him. I dropped my bag in the seat next to yours and strode up to the podium, where Samuelson was reviewing his notes. I hadn't heard back when I e-mailed him "I'm Nobody! Who Are You?: The Self as Staffage in Emily Dickinson," so I'd printed out a hard copy. "In case this got lost in your in-box," I said, handing it to him.

He held the pages at a distance and lifted his head to read the type through his bifocals. "Your paper?" He tried to give it back to me. "You're supposed to send this to your section leader."

"I know," I said. "I e-mailed it to Harriet, of course. I just thought

you might also want to read it, because of last time. It's not on Hawthorne, but I figured that can wait till next semester."

Samuelson looked bewildered and a little peeved. "What happened last time?"

"Never mind," I said, taking the paper from him. *I* was the one who
should have been annoyed. To have cited a student's essay in class and
invited him to office hours, only to forget him altogether, wasn't just
absentminded; it was disrespectful. When I returned to my seat, you
were looking at your phone, kindly pretending to be too preoccupied
to have registered the failed exchange. Samuelson began, your device
vanished, your notebook came out, and you struck a pose of intense
concentration that you maintained for the duration of his talk.

"If nothing else," Samuelson said in his concluding remarks, "I hope
I've done you all the wonderful service of making you aware of your
own tragic flaws." There was polite laughter and a round of applause.

"So your friend's okay?" I asked you as the clapping petered out.

You nodded as you packed up but didn't volunteer any details.

"Glad to hear it," I said. "My friends showed up right after you
left, so I didn't know if I should give them your drinks, or what. I
guess I should've explained that in my messages."

"No worries." You shouldered your bag and turned toward the aisle.

"I was planning on knocking my final paper out of the way this
week," I said as we waited for the aisle bottleneck to clear. "Want to
meet up?"

"I'm pretty busy with other work this week."

"Next week's good, too. I'm flexible."

You took your phone and earbuds out of your bag. "Don't wait
on my account."

"No, you're right, I've got other finals I should take care of first."
You untangled the cord.

"So just let me know when you're ready to meet," I said.

"Will do."

"Cool. I'll wait for you to get in touch." As we stepped into the hall you put the earbuds in. "One more thing," I said in a hushed tone, and subtly nodded my head back to the classroom.

Your eyes flitted around us, indicating you knew what I was about to bring up and that we shouldn't discuss it in the open, especially not with Tom nearby. Your signal was unnecessary: you could trust me not to blurt out anything confidential.

"Do you need any help?" I whispered.

"I'm taking care of it," you said casually.

"Remember, you can bring me along as a personal advisor. Or if you just need moral support."

You waited for the group ahead of us to move on. "They actually told me I shouldn't be discussing it. So the best thing you could do for me is to respect that."

"Got it." I nodded. "Well, keep me posted."

"No, you don't get it," you said. "I'm asking you—I'm *tell*ing you, this conversation is over. I can't be talking about this with *anyone*." You looked straight into my eyes. "Do you read me?"

Od uoy daer em?

"Of course," I said. "I completely understand." I bet no one else knew about it, not even Suzanne. Only me.

Reading period commenced a few days later. An unstructured week to study before the rude arrival of finals, its longueurs felt like a never-ending Sunday afternoon. My room was devoid of activity; Steven had begun a codependent relationship with the one female member of his magic club and alighted at home only for changes of clothes. The library was crowded with students who flocked to the communal tables like pigeons to bread crumbs. Even sequestered in the privacy of a carrel, I found it difficult to focus; the floor and walls seemed to vibrate with the buzz of their prattling. I brought my work to Annenberg, where I continued to dine solo, a quarantined patient. The social fluidity of September had frozen into compartmentalized ice cubes; fixed units of freshmen, strangers a short three months ago, now bantered with the glib repartee of news anchors between segments.

I didn't see you at any meals, but a lot of students were skipping them to prepare for finals.

And so what; I'd have you to myself soon enough, after the last essay had brought us closer together. The others were movie extras, background noise. Pure staffage in our landscape.

One evening Scott Tupper cut ahead of me in line for soda. I let it go, but an hour later, back in my room, I set up a fake e-mail account and wrote an anonymous, scathing character assassination, telling him one of his childhood victims knew where he lived.

I couldn't find his e-mail address in the student directory. Searching for him on Facebook didn't turn up anyone in the Harvard network, either. There was a guy with his name associated with the University of Vermont, though. I clicked on the profile.

It was Scott.

He looked similar to the pug-nosed guy at Harvard, just with longish hair. But the real Scott Tupper, as his Facebook page would have you believe, had become a budding left-wing intellectual; his interests included Marx and Noam Chomsky, and all the links he posted were to articles about social justice and the evils of corporate influence.

Naturally he'd be going to a state school.

I received back my graded "I'm Nobody! Who Are You?: The Self as Staffage in Emily Dickinson" essay. The sentences were massacred with red ink. "Some interesting insights, but an incoherent argument," my TF had written on the last page. "B–."

My first B. Not just at Harvard (where I'd been pulling off As and A minuses), but in my entire academic career. I'd rather have gotten an F. Absolute failure could be indicative of unappreciated genius. Mediocrity wasn't.

It was because I'd put all my best thinking into *your* paper. Fortunately, there was still the final essay. This time I'd prioritize my own work to prove that the B minus was a fluke, that I was indeed one of the most gifted students Mrs. Rice had encountered in her twenty-four years teaching English at Garret Hobart High. I decided to write about the troika of *The Sun Also Rises*, *The Great Gatsby*, and the course's namesake poem, furiously banging out pages of shorthand ideas about Europe and America, old money and new money, gentiles and Jews, the plainspokenness of Hemingway as masculine cover for his cerebral vocation, Fitzgerald's lyricism and Eliot's classicism as a doubling down on their effeteness.

But when I tried to compose the first draft, I struggled to transform my notes into a coherent argument, let alone a cogent, nuanced one executed in a fancy prose style. To procrastinate, I ended up translating the complete document of stray thoughts in reverse. I encountered a similar block for my other classes' essays, too. All I could think about was how, once I saw you again, we would pick up on what we'd done that night in my room.

I roamed around the River Houses one night until I heard the sounds of a party. I waited until a resident opened the door, followed the music, and entered the congested suite. There wasn't anyone I recognized. I stood by the alcohol, refilling each cup as soon as I'd emptied it, and stayed till the end. No one spoke to me.

Reading week was drawing to a close and you hadn't reached out yet to schedule our next session. I e-mailed you:

Just checking in about when you wanted to work on our Prufrock essays together. I'm free whenever.

I stayed up until four in the morning waiting for your reply. It wasn't there when I awoke at noon, either. Maybe you were neglecting your in-box as you took care of finals. Nonetheless, it was inconsiderate. I was offering my services; you could at least have had the courtesy to tell me when you were available.

I needed to run into you on campus. But I hadn't seen you in the dining hall the whole week, and I couldn't stand by your room, obviously. I would have to intercept you before or after one of your exams.

I checked the syllabus for Gender and the Consumerist Impulse. In lieu of an exam was a final paper (the "anthropological study requiring local fieldwork") due in your professor's mailbox that day by five o'clock. It was already 2:30 but, knowing you, you'd hand it in under the wire; I could linger by the mailboxes, pretending I was there for some other purpose.

I jogged over to Boylston Hall, found the correct mailbox, and sifted through the essays to confirm that yours wasn't there yet. But it was—near the top of the stack:

A QUID PRO QUO:
A Market-Based Study of Fe(male) Sexual Transactions
by Veronica Wells

If only I'd remembered the syllabus an hour earlier, I would've been there when you dropped it off. The one consolation was that I could now read what you'd written: "sexual transactions" sounded intriguing.

Students and faculty trickled by, all consumed with their own urgent end-of-semester business. I snatched the paper and hurried downstairs to the basement, avoiding the dangerous space of the BGLTQ lounge, and cloistered myself in a stall in the men's room.

"If love does not know how to give and take without restrictions, it is not love, but a transaction that never fails to lay stress on a plus and a minus."

—Emma Goldman, "The Tragedy of
Woman's Emancipation" (1906)

Introduction

Though Hollywood would have us believe that all we seek in romantic relationships is love, it is just one of several exchangeable commodities, along with sex, money, status, validation, services, and so on. While I have long been aware of—and troubled by— the transactional nature of relationships, I have been as susceptible to this dynamic as anyone else.

On September 4, I became acquainted with a male member of Harvard's senior class ("Alpha"). There was a mutual attraction and we began dating. Within a few weeks, the terms of the transaction were glaringly apparent. Aware of his high market value in the heteronormative undergraduate social economy, Alpha conducted himself in a manner suggesting that his status and finances would satisfy all my relationship needs.

They did not; I found the relationship lacking in several crucial respects. Rather than extricate myself, however, I decided to study it through an anthropological and economic lens. As part of this exploration, I have included a log of our noteworthy interactions, the money Alpha spent on me, and our sexual encounters (intercourse, fellatio, and/or cunnilingus). An annotated analysis of the transactions composes Part 2 of this study, in which I consider which commodities influence the power dynamic of a relationship; how each partner calculates the costs

and benefits of a given transaction; and the transactional relationships among money, sex, and status.

Part 1: Beta

A few days into my study of Alpha, I became acquainted with
a freshman male ("Beta"). On October 5, he offered to help me
work on an essay due in a class we shared. I realized that I did
not have a comparison subject for Alpha, who was receiving various commodities from me, just as I was from him. What if I
entered into a Platonic relationship with a lower-value male that
exclusively benefited me? To what lengths would Beta extend
himself for the presumptive possibility of sex? How might it re-
fract the power dynamic between Alpha and me?

I expanded the ambit of my study to include Beta. With no
suggestions on my end of sexual reward, he voluntarily wrote two
essays for me in clear violation of the Honor Code.[1] Despite the
fact that we were not in a sexual relationship, Beta began to act in
much the same entitled, possessive manner as Alpha, subjecting
me to disturbing levels of surveillance in a number of episodes.
A more thorough examination of our relationship is in Part 3.

Beta's behavior in the early stages made me uneasy, and I
attempted to end our association prior to the second essay he
wrote for me; in spite of this, he was adamant about maintaining
it. But after an incident in which he followed me around New
York City, I felt unsafe in his presence and withdrew from him
before his expectation of sex became unmanageable.

---

[1] I wrote my own papers before our meetings and did not, of course,
submit either of his, which suffered from retrograde ideas and
stilted prose, as if he thought he could browbeat me into admiring
submission with overwrought sentence constructions and baroque
vocabulary.

Insert an empty page for my restroom-stall silence, printer.

My thighs atrophied. I sat down on the toilet seat before reading the rest, which was more of the same. Then I reread the whole thing. Each time my eyes passed over the word *Beta*, it was as if an organ were surgically extracted from me without anesthesia and deposited on the operating table so I could witness my own vivisection.

Someone entered the restroom, unzipped, urinated, whistled, zipped, flushed, turned on the faucet, turned off the faucet, crank-crank-cranked the paper-towel dispenser, ripped, dried, tossed it in the trash, and left to go on with his day—his world as intact upon departure as it was on arrival.

I struggled to stand; my legs had fallen asleep. The pins and needles were the only sign that I was still inhabiting my body, which seemed to belong to another person wobbling in the narrow stall.

Feet tingling, essay in pocket, I left the building. It was barely four o'clock but the streetlights were already on, the sky a metallic pink as the first flurry of the season fell, ashen flakes that melted upon contact with the ground. I was walking back to Matthews when I realized I didn't want to be in my room, didn't want to be on campus at all, so I turned south through the tranquil Yard and into the bustle of Harvard Square, past storefronts winking with Christmas lights, past two kids sticking out their tongues to catch the snowflakes, past a Salvation Army Santa Claus ringing a bell, past a fire truck with a wreath on the grill ambling down Mass Ave.

Beta. That's all I was to you. Beta. That's all I was.

No particular destination in mind, I kept walking. Halfway across the Anderson Memorial Bridge, I paused to read a small plaque embedded in the brick wall.

QUENTIN COMPSON
Drowned in the odour
of honeysuckle
1891–1910

A fictional character had left more of a literal mark on this place than I ever would.

DAVID FEDERMAN
Wasn't here
August–December

Freezing gusts of winter unfurled off the river. I opened up the contacts on my phone. No need to scroll; the entire list fit on one screen: Anna, Dad, Miriam, Mom, Sara Cohen.

"David, hi, I'm in the middle of something. Can I swing by your office in five?" answered my mother.

"Mom?" I said, confused. "It's me. David."

"Oh!" She laughed. "I saw your name and thought it was David Franklin at my firm. I didn't call you, did I?"

"No."

"Well, it's nice to hear your voice." Her keyboard clacked in the background. "How're finals?"

"Fine," I said.

Rustling papers. "Busy studying?"

"Mmhuh."

"It sounds windy. Are you outside?"

"Just taking a little break outside the library."

"Thank you."

"For what?"

"Sorry, I was talking to someone else. I hope you're not too stressed out."

"I'm not. I'm about to meet my friends for dinner."

"Oh, good," she said. "What do you call yourselves, again? The Matthews Martyrs?"

"Marauders."

"Of course, the *Marauders.*" She laughed again. "Excuse me."

"I should probably get going," I said.

"Okay," she said. "Remind me what day you're taking the bus?"

I didn't answer.

"David? I can't hear you."

My breathing became jerky. I moved the phone away from my mouth.

"You still there?"

"I'm here," I said, my voice catching in my throat.

"*David,*" she said in a tone she hadn't used since I was a child. "Are you crying? Did something happen?"

"There's this girl." I choked on the rest of the sentence.

"A girl?" She waited. "Is it a *girlfriend*?"

"No," I said. "She didn't want to be."

"Oh, David," she clucked. "I'm so sorry. I wish I could reach through the phone right now and give you a hug."

The skyline slackened and quivered. The lights dancing off the river blurred into a shiny nimbus.

"I know it's hard to believe this, because it feels awful now, but you'll get over it," she said. "I was so heartbroken over this boy my freshman year of college, I hardly ate for weeks. And now I can't even remember his name!"

The snow began sticking. The squeak of windshield wipers could be heard as traffic slowed.

"Have you talked about this with your friends?" she asked.

When I didn't answer she continued. "I know you're a private person, but it's important not to let these things simmer inside. This might sound silly, but I read an article that said if you're upset with someone, a good thing to do is write them a letter expressing your feelings, but don't send it. Just for yourself. It can help you get closure."

I wiped my nose on my sleeve and blinked the world back into focus.

"Did I lose you?" she asked.

I cleared my throat and filled my lungs with cold, clarifying air.

"That's a good idea," I said, heading back to campus. "Closure."

Chapter 16

I feel like we left things a little unresolved," I began. "I was hoping to get some closure."

"How generous of you to include me," Sara said.

It had taken four days of e-mails to persuade her to meet me; on top of her reasons for not wanting to see me again, finals were now upon us. But she had at last consented to talk, briefly, in a public location.

We sat at our usual table at Starbucks. "Rudolph the Red-Nosed Reindeer" jingled over the café's sound system. Our drinks steamed from festively decorated cups. A toddler parked in a stroller at the next table rooted through a shopping bag at her feet while her mother vertically caressed the screen of her phone.

"I don't blame you for being mad at me," I went on. "I've given it a lot of thought, and I've come to realize you were right."

Sara leaned back, crossed her arms, and let out a skeptical sigh.

"About something being wrong with me," I said. "There is. Sort of."

Her forehead crinkled in confusion.

"You said I was missing whatever it is that makes someone feel things for other people," I reminded her. "But it's there—it's just hard to see, sometimes even for me. Underneath this affectless exterior lies a deeply sensitive being."

She rolled her eyes. "Oh, please."

"That's your line," I said. "At the Ice Cream Bash. Except you said pleasant exterior and antisocial being. Then you made a joke about being a psychopath."

"Right." A reluctant nod. "You have a good memory."

"About us," I said. "I remember everything. All the plays and lectures you took me to. Our study sessions at Lamont, and here. Our first date, at that salsa class. When we danced so beautifully."

A twitch of a smile. I pressed on.

"The very first time I met you, outside Matthews. You picked up my orientation packet that had fallen and you had sunscreen all over your face. Then you came over to say hello in the basement meeting, but I was too nervous to talk."

The toddler next to us howled in protest as her mother pried a new pair of socks from her hands. She was quickly pacified with a cookie the size of her face.

"The other reason I wanted to meet is there's something I need to say to you," I said. "Something I wasn't up front about that's been weighing on my conscience. It's not easy for me to talk about this, but you deserve to know."

Sara looked soberly into her coffee.

"I lied about not being a virgin," I said. "I was insecure, and I think I overcompensated and did things with you, in bed, that I felt weird about after. I want to apologize."

Sara tore off the sleeve of her cup and ran her fingers along the ribbed interior. "Listen, David. I didn't mean what I said about you not feelings things. That just came out in the heat of the moment. The breakup caught me off guard, and on top of being painful, it was a real slap in the face. You weren't always the easiest boyfriend.

You could be remote, and there were times when it was hard to get through your defenses. That was okay, though—I figured it was worth the effort to get whatever was in there out. But I thought we were finally getting somewhere."

"We were!" I cut in. "That's what's been driving me crazy. If only I'd shared more of myself. I feel like I missed out on something really meaningful with you. And I know I'll regret that for a long time— thinking about what could have been, and the feeling that I threw it away."

Her eyes rose to meet mine. "I'm new to the whole relationship business," she said, "but the way I see it, there's no point in beating yourself up for what you did or didn't do in the past. Each experience teaches us something about ourselves, and you take what you learn to the next relationship, and you're the better for it. I know it sounds corny, but I really do believe this."

"I don't want another relationship."

She laughed. "Oh, David. I wouldn't allow what happened between us to turn you off girls forever. It's not like this was a thirty-year marriage that just collapsed. We're in our first semester of college. This is *supposed* to happen."

"That's not what I mean," I said. "I'm not interested in a new relationship. I want to go back to the last one."

Sara's nostrils flared as she took a contemplative breath.

"I don't know what to say," she told me after a protracted silence. "I wasn't expecting this, and it's a lot to think about. I can't give you a definitive answer right now, if that's what you're looking for. Maybe we can talk more after the break."

"Of course. Of course." I took the first, cautious sip of my piping-hot coffee. "Well, how'd your finals go?"

Her face softened in amusement. "Really? *That's* your transition?"

"You know better than anyone that small talk has never been my forte," I said.

She smiled. "Yeah, I forgot. Three classes down, one to go. I won't bore you with the details. How are yours going?"

"Same here." I'd skipped my economics exam and still hadn't written the final papers for my other classes. "Anything else new?"

"Not much," she said. "Oh—except Layla's moving in."

"With you?"

"Yeah, she's taking Veronica's place."

I took a swig of coffee and let it scald the roof of my mouth.

"When did this happen?"

"Veronica just told me she was moving out two days ago," Sara said. "Layla doesn't like her roommate, either, so we asked the housing office if she could move in with me, and they approved it."

"Is she moving into Layla's room?"

"No. She was weirdly cagey when I asked where she was going. All I know is she *hired* someone to move her stuff tomorrow morning. Who does that in *college*?" She waited for a reaction. "I shouldn't be so catty. She looked a little embarrassed when she told me."

"So just one more night with her, huh?" I asked.

"Yeah, and she actually has to spend the night for once, since the movers are coming at *seven* in the morning. My room's going to be a war zone for the next twenty-four hours: Layla's flying home tomorrow and she's in exams all day today, so *she's* got to move tonight." She checked the time on her phone. "That reminds me, I have to pick up a key for her at the housing office before it closes."

"A key?"

"For the room." She waved her hand in front of my face. "Earth to David. You there?"

"Yeah," I said. "Well, that's great news. It'll be nice to have a roommate who's a good person."

"I wouldn't call Veronica a *bad* person. I feel sort of sorry for her. She seems a bit tormented."

"I don't know about tormented. I got the sense that she's just not that nice."

"The gentleman doth protest too much."

"Why do you say that?"

"I don't know," she said with a shrug. "You always got kind of antsy when she was around. I guess I wondered if you had a little crush."

I made a face.

"A harmless crush," she qualified. "I mean, what guy wouldn't, from a distance?"

"So you're helping Layla move tonight?"

"No—I feel awful about it, but I have my final evening session with my students to go over their college essays. Maybe I'll be able to pitch in at the end when I get back."

"Is anyone helping her?"

She shook her head. "And we're supposed to get six inches of snow tonight."

"I could lend a hand," I said.

"You don't have to do that."

"I'd be glad to. I don't really have anything else to do."

Someone called out "David!" Sara and I both turned our heads, but it was just the barista letting a customer know his drink was ready.

"Well, if you're serious, that's a very generous offer," Sara said. "Layla always liked you."

We got up to leave. Sara waved good-bye to the little girl next to us. She beamed back at her and held out the soggy remains of her cookie as a parting gift.

"That's so nice of you," Sara told her. "It looks delicious, but I have to save room for dinner."

I met up with Layla that evening and, load by load, we transported her belongings from her dorm to Matthews, stacking her boxes in neat rows in Sara's room and leaving an aisle for your own move in the morning. The whole process took about two hours, throughout which your window remained dark and no sounds issued from your room. As we returned to Layla's dorm for the final trip, it started to snow. There were two boxes left, and I told her I could handle them on my own.

"Don't be silly," I said when she insisted on helping. "You have an early flight tomorrow. Stay here. I've got this."

"You sure?"

"Of course." I picked up the boxes, creating a small tower that blocked my face. "Oh, whoops—I forgot the key. Duh."

My hands full, she dropped the room key in the pocket of my parka and held the door for me. "Back soon," I said.

I hauled the boxes over to Sara's room. On the way back I detached my room key from my key chain and replaced it with Layla's. "Here you go," I said, handing her my own key.

"Thank you so much, David," she said, marveling at the bareness of her room. "I don't know how I would've done this alone. You really are a nice guy."

"Not at all," I said.

Sara would be getting home soon. I dashed back through the Yard to Matthews, nearly slipping on the snow-slick pavement, and let myself into room 505 with Layla's key. I pressed my ear against your door and heard nothing. The light was still off. I was confident you were out, though it was remotely possible you had come in during Layla's move and gone to sleep early. Holding my breath, I cracked the door open.

Orange lamplight from the Yard pooled in, glazing a dozen or so boxes haphazardly scattered about the room. Your bed was empty.

The closet was cleared out. I reached into the interior pocket of my parka and removed my phone, your essay, and the bathrobe belt. I took off the parka, along with my jeans and shoes, and put them on the top shelf. Then I stepped inside and shut the door.

I sat cross-legged on the floor, knees resting against the walls, and reread your essay by the light of my phone.

All that time I thought I'd just been watching you, and it turned

out you'd been keeping close tabs on me, too. It was almost flatter-
ing.

But there were omissions: no mention of the elbow contact
during lecture, of crying in my arms on the stairs, of flirting with me
outside Sara's room. Certainly nothing about the picture frame. You
were as dishonest in your "study" as you'd been with me all along.
Your icebreaker descriptor should have been *inveritas*.

I touched your bathrobe belt. You had no idea that I'd taken it
or what I'd done with it—countless times. Add *that* to Part 3 of your
essay.

Around nine o'clock I heard something. I darkened my phone
and sat perfectly still. The door swung closed in the other room.
I waited for the sound of your door opening. A minute passed—it
must have been Sara. Moments later my phone silently lit up with a
text from her:

> I stopped by your room to thank you for helping Layla but
> you weren't home. There's a pizza study break in the basement.
> Thinking of going if you want to join.

I switched my phone off; I needed to stay alert. To pass the time,
I balled up your belt in my hand and squeezed it, relaxed my fingers,
let it spill out, and rolled it up to compress it again. Eventually I
heard the muted purr of Sara's white-noise machine. Through two
sets of doors it sounded like the comforting whoosh of a distant
highway.

I periodically turned my phone back on to see the time. The
final check was at 1:43 a.m. Shortly after this I heard footsteps and
a creak. A subtle air current rattled the closet door. The space between the floor and the door filled with light. A clomp and a thump,
what sounded like coins dropping, a cross between a grunt and a
sigh, then the light turned off and it was quiet again. No bathroom
routine tonight.

You were tipsy if not intoxicated. In a few minutes you'd be out cold. I waited that long, plus a little more, twisting the belt and knotting it this time so it retained the shape of a ball. Then I rotated the knob slowly and fully—so as not to make a clicking sound—and nudged the closet door ajar.

You'd neglected to pull down the shades; the light from outside illuminated the rhythmic rise and fall of the white comforter, its contours forming a snowcapped, undulating mountain range. You weren't snoring, but you took husky breaths, the stertorous sleep of the inebriated.

I skied soundlessly across the floor in my socks, slaloming around your boots, peacoat, and jeans, until I arrived at your bed. Your black sweater statically clung to the side of the comforter. A bottle of pills was uncapped on your bedside table; the Ambien you needed so desperately to fall asleep. You lay on your back, hair feathered across the pillow as if floating underwater, lips parted, face slack.

I left the knotted belt on your bedside table.

Reaching over your body, I lifted the top of the comforter, careful not to create a breeze as I peeled its downy bulk off the length of you. The sheet was twisted at the foot of the bed.

A gossamer T-shirt hugged your torso. Your legs were bare, but you wore underpants.

An abrupt breath was chased by a spluttery snore. I waited for you to settle before proceeding. Pinching either side of the elastic waistband, I coaxed the underpants down, past the barrier of your backside and the mattress, across your thighs, over the hillocks of your knees, along your shins, and off your ankles.

Your winter-pale body stretched out before me like a patient etherized upon a table. *It would be wonderful if David shared his observations more in class with his peers, who would surely benefit.* A delicate band of crenellations snaked around your hips. A trim delta of hair over your mons pubis.

Despite your half nakedness, I wasn't aroused. I took off my boxers and fondled myself, but remained inert. Foiled by my own pathetic phallus.

Yet when I looked up at the tender hollow below your throat where the sloping clavicles nearly met, a cove for a locket, I felt a tingling. I held a hand over your neck, so close that I could feel the heat of your skin. My quiescent penis rose phoenixlike; where there had been a noodle was now a saber. (Is my prose too stilted for you, my sentence constructions overwrought, my vocabulary baroque, my register phallogocentric?)

I stood there, fisting the bathrobe belt, summoning my resolve.

And then it was happening: I was mounting the mattress, my knees were straddling your parallel legs, I was burrowing my fingers into the crevice between your thighs, gently separating them.

"Who—" you said groggily, your eyelids fluttering.

No sense in delicacy now. I pushed your legs akimbo and maneuvered my knees between them.

"David!" you rasped, your palms meekly protesting my gravity.

"Veronica."

The first time I'd ever said your name aloud; I thought of it constantly but it seemed too sacred to speak.

You screamed. When I tried to plug your mouth with the silk ball, you bit me. On the second scream I got it inside. I pinned down your arms as you wriggled and gagged.

How unjust the world is that some people can buy, on consumerist impulse, silk bathrobe belts with their initials on them and some people can buy them only without initials and some people can't buy them at all.

You continued thrashing to no avail, my arms becoming someone else's more muscular arms, my legs doubling in size, my body lengthening and massing as you shrank in direct proportion under me. But this is how you wanted me to act all along, isn't it.

Before I could penetrate you, I heard a second set of female vocals.

The door was open and Sara was clawing my back. One of your knees squirmed free in the turmoil and uppercut me between my legs. I toppled to the side of the bed like a timbered tree, whimpering and clutching myself, quickly reduced to a flaccid state. A mushroom cloud of pain swelled through my gut.

When I looked up, I was the only one in the room. I instinctively put on my jeans and sneakers and hobbled out to Sara's bedroom, pausing by the door to the hallway. Alarmed voices.

I collected my thoughts, reminded myself of the original plan. Fleeing was for the cowardly and deceitful. For the weak. You were the one who'd fled. The heroic manifested their own destinies and accepted their undeserved punishments without complaint.

I staggered back through the narrow passage lined by Layla's boxes and returned to your room. En route to the bed I picked your black sweater off the floor and slipped it on. Pulling the comforter up, I waited for the authorities. The bed was warm and smelled of you.

DAVID FEDERMAN
Drowned in the odour
of Veronica

I was rousted from the bed and manacled. "You have the right to remain silent," an officer barked, *uoy evah eht thgir ot niamer tnelis.* I ignored the rest and was paraded out through the hall and downstairs past Matthews residents peeping from the safety of their rooms.

A few police cars idled in the Yard, where a small crowd of spectators had assembled. It was still snowing. They shivered in pajamas and coats, their sleep interrupted during finals: perfect little Harvard students, I was once like all of them.

"Oh, my God," said a girl who lived two rooms down (Cecily Trimmer, Houston, Texas). The cops bowed my head and pushed me into the backseat of a car. "He's *right* on my hall."

The cinematic montage of my future unspooled before me. The media would pounce. The front page of the *Crimson* would report daily updates on my case, gathering quotes from Steven. (" 'I guess he was a little strange—he never really wanted to hang out,' observed the alleged assailant's roommate, Steven G. Zenger.") National coverage would follow with sensationalistic psychological profiles. Old acquaintances would come forth; *I knew him,* they'd say, *seemed harmless, pretty quiet, I think he once said my name backward or something.* There would be round-the-clock cable news updates, vociferous op-eds about sexual assault in college, and agenda-serving think pieces holding me up as a metaphor for a panoply of societal disorders. A British tabloid would give me the libelous sobriquet "the Harvard Rapist"; the Parisian press would speculate about a ménage à trois gone wrong. The frozen, lopsided smile from my *Freshman Register* photo would fuel their fascination. The white male with whom everyone would become obsessed.

I would listen, deadpan, as the foreman read the jury's decision in my televised trial for attempted rape. A verdict of guilty for the Harvard Rapist, David Alan Federman. Famous David.

None of that happened.

The burden of proof was on you, and aside from your police report and the eyewitness account of a jilted ex-girlfriend, the only damning evidence was a paper you'd written (not approved by your professor, it turned out, who disavowed the topic and research protocol as academically unethical) that showed you'd manipulated me. I had planned to employ the belt, my parents' colleague would argue, for sadomasochistic purposes during consensual sex, and you had reacted hysterically once we began. My clothes were in the closet to separate them from your belongings ready to be moved. We had been seen at final clubs together on multiple occasions looking friendly with each other if not intimate; the only time I had shown up anywhere unexpected was in New York City, at a public venue, a mere coincidence. And if Sara testified, he would question why, if I'd supposedly been aggressive in bed, she had sent me a text saying she was thinking of me.

The Harvard connection would make it a high-profile trial, and your name—plus those of your prominent parents—would inevitably leak out. My lawyer also suggested that, should we go to court, allegations about your cocaine use and an affair with a married graduate student would be forthcoming.

The district attorney, afraid of losing the case, convinced your publicity-wary parents that it would be best for everyone if I were allowed to plead guilty to a lesser offense, assault and battery, sentencing to be held five years later, with the understanding that as long as I didn't harass you in any way, physically or verbally, then my case would be dismissed, all pertaining material would be sealed, I wouldn't have to register as a sex offender, and—

To put it in layman's terms, I'd get off scot-free.

I told my parents I wanted my day in court, to clear my name completely and (I didn't mention this part) to tarnish yours. Absolutely not, they said; it wasn't worth the possibility of not winning.

From what I heard, you were initially outraged by the terms of the plea bargain, but upon learning that the Ad Board was kicking me out of Harvard, you grudgingly agreed. My parents instructed me not to appeal the decision, assuring me I could transfer to another good school the next year. I went along with everything.

The *Crimson* reported on the incident (using only my name) and my expulsion but, lacking juicy details and a court case, soon turned its attention to a hazing scandal at a final club.

With my academic rap sheet, however, no respectable institution would accept me. My parents insisted I go somewhere, so I enrolled at a community college within driving distance of home. I got meaningless straight As without even trying, took my cafeteria lunches outside. An English composition adjunct said I showed a lot of academic promise and should consider applying to a four-year school.

Word spread to my Hobart High classmates. "I guess you decided not to take it slow after all!" Daniel Hallman e-mailed me. That was the last I heard from anyone there.

Anna hardly acknowledged me. When Miriam came home, she chose her words carefully, as if I were an obtuse foreigner.

I don't leave the house much these days. Usually I'm in my bedroom, on the Internet. You can burn a great deal of hours like that.

I turned twenty-four last week. My mother asked if I wanted anything special for my birthday. To get my van Gogh prints framed, I said. She also gave me a pair of slippers with *DAF* monogrammed across the toes.

It's risky to do anything with this, even if there aren't judicial consequences. You wouldn't read it anyhow; you were never interested in knowing me. But I didn't write it for you (the way you manipulated me to write your essays, the way you manipulated me the whole time). I wrote it *about* you, a big prepositional difference. For legal purposes, let's classify it as fiction—or as fictional as your term paper. Call it *Veronica Morgan Wells: A Study*.

It's funny. Lately I've found myself thinking of Sara more often than I do of you. The other day I saw she had a new profile photo, one of her and a guy hiking through some woods, their backs to the camera.

I couldn't see her other pictures, but I imagined what she looked like now, and began conjuring her future selves as the years whipped by and she accumulated wrinkles and pounds and reading glasses. Also kids and a husband—me, with thinning hair and a thickening waist, the two of us racking mugs and bowls in the dishwasher, scooting our brood off to school, a hectic morning routine; but before we departed for our idealistic jobs that actually existed, she kissed me good-bye, tapping me on the head twice.

Knock, knock. Who's in there?

We shared a smile, the kind couples reserve for private jokes that no longer inspire laughter but still bear the memory of it, because, after all these years together, she had gotten me to let whatever was in there out.

In Harvard Yard that winter night—more than five years ago—I settled into the police car, my posture slumped from the handcuffs, red and blue lights flashing around me like Fourth of July fireworks.

"What's his name?" one of the gawking students asked the girl down my hall. "Who is he?"

I sat up, my spine erect against the seat, making myself more visible, listening for my name.

Divad Namredef. Somewhat of a loner.

"I don't know," she said, and the door closed.

Acknowledgments

I am grateful to the following:

my two editors—Millicent Bennett, to whom I am profoundly indebted for her meticulous attention and unflagging stamina, and Ira Silverberg, as adroit a shepherd and champion as I could ask for; their respective assistants, Julianna Haubner and Kaitlin Olson; my superb publicist, Erin Reback; my copy editor, David Chesanow; and Jon Karp, Marysue Rucci, and everyone else at Simon & Schuster;

my agent, Jim Rutman, a paragon of professionalism and decency;

my selfless and perspicacious readers—Chelsea Bieker, Clara Boyd, Sarah Bruni, Amber Dermont, Maura Kelly, Aryn Kyle, Diana Spechler, and John Warner;

my research resources—Andrew Epstein in clinical psychology, Josh Gradinger in the law, and Julian Lucas for Harvard-related queries (all errors are mine);

for conversations on the subjects of risk and reward, Lev Moscow and Nathaniel Popper;

the MacDowell Colony and the Sewanee Writers' Conference;

the Greathead/Pennoyer family for welcoming me so warmly, and the Waynes for not evicting me;

and, finally, Kate Greathead, who not only tirelessly and sacrificially took time to make this novel the best possible version of itself, but has even more generously done the same for me.

About the Author

Teddy Wayne is the author of two previous novels, *The Love Song of Jonny Valentine* and *Kapitoil.* He is the winner of a Whiting Writers' Award and an NEA Creative Writing Fellowship, as well as a finalist for the Young Lions Fiction Award, PEN/Bingham Prize, and Dayton Literary Peace Prize. A columnist for *The New York Times,* he is a regular contributor to *The New Yorker, Vanity Fair,* and *McSweeney's,* and has taught at Columbia University and Washington University in St. Louis. He lives in New York.